Books by Margery Sharp

RHODODENDRON PIE
FANFARE FOR TIN TRUMPETS
THE FLOWERING THORN
FOUR GARDENS
THE NUTMEG TREE
THE STONE OF CHASTITY
THREE COMPANION PIECES
CLUNY BROWN
BRITANNIA MEWS
THE FOOLISH GENTLEWOMAN
LISE LILLYWHITE
THE GIPSY IN THE PARLOUR
THE EYE OF LOVE
SOMETHING LIGHT
MARTHA IN PARIS
MARTHA, ERIC AND GEORGE
THE SUN IN SCORPIO
IN PIOUS MEMORY
ROSA
THE INNOCENTS

THE RESCUERS
MISS BIANCA
THE TURRET
LOST AT THE FAIR
MISS BIANCA IN THE SALT MINES
MISS BIANCA IN THE ORIENT
MISS BIANCA IN THE ANTARCTIC

THE INNOCENTS

THE
INNOCENTS

BY MARGERY SHARP

LITTLE, BROWN AND COMPANY
BOSTON—TORONTO

PART
ONE

1

My father was a connoisseur of wine; but times and incomes change and we with them, and now I am a connoisseur of weather. Thus I remember distinctly the day of Cecilia's return as being cool (for mid-April), but not cold; showery rather than rainy, also with a peculiar tang in the air (which I have noticed as late as May) that seems to presage not summer but autumn. Oddly enough, the day she died some five months later, in October, had a rather springlike feeling — though this of course may have been subconscious on my part.

How fortunate the connoisseur of weather who is born English! When I say the intervening summer was unusually fine I do not by any means describe such a succession of monotonously cloudy days as they have to put up with in Kenya, for instance, or in India — before the equally predictable and monotonous Rains. In England, and particularly in East Anglia, a single afternoon may embrace several meteorological extremes, especially if there is an Outdoor Fête. The sensation of voile clinging damply to the skin is almost a birthright!

Not that Cecilia ever wore voile. We all knew, as in a village everyone knows everything, that her late parents couldn't have left her much beyond the small house in the High Street, but she had turned the downstairs part into a very nice dress shop and no doubt got trade prices: at all Outdoor Fêtes Cecilia in her tailored silk suits was so conspicuously elegant, on one occasion a child presented her with the bouquet destined for its titled Patroness. Cecilia made a great joke of it — as she said, how could she possibly abash the innocent by refusing, or even passing on, the booty? So it was Cecilia, not Lady A., who strolled through the afternoon badged by a dozen pink carnations!

I personally have never cared for carnations of any colour. They are too much of a florist's flower. Outdoors they always look either disheveled, or (if individually sticked) stiff.

What I should have perhaps mentioned about Cecilia at once was that she was a beauty. Her colouring was pure East Anglian, and our young girls are unsurpassable for abundant russet hair and glowing, peaches-and-cream complexions; only they tend to put on weight quite enormously, particularly below the waist, till they soon look like our neighbouring Norfolk's dumplings. Cecilia at twenty-seven had legs long and slim as a heron's; she was tall for a woman altogether, and height matched her wonderfully clear-cut features; it seemed right that so lovely a head should be carried high. I have never seen a more beautiful woman, and like everyone else sometimes felt surprise that she wasn't married. However it was by her own choice; half the bachelors of the neighbourhood had proposed to Cecilia in their time, but whether gentleman-farmer, or curate, or solicitor, or once the County Surveyor and once a Bank Manager, she turned them all down, and again in their time they married someone else. Of course she had a right to be difficult!—and if some ungenerous tongue occasionally remarked that she wasn't getting any younger, one had only to look at her to see the implication not only unkind but absurd. As I never beheld a more beautiful girl, so, I repeat, I have never beheld a more beautiful woman — and nor apparently had Rab (or Robert) Guthrie.

2

How far more appreciative and careful of family ties are the Scots, and particularly the American-Scots, than we British! I myself have a brother with a parish in Cornwall whom I visit no more often than he does me; Robert Guthrie crossed the Atlantic to see a mere cousin — our own Tam (or Thomas) of Leys Farm, who'd flighted no farther than Suffolk, where indeed he so Scottishly prospered, his wife if he'd had one would have been opening Fêtes right and left. But like his transatlantic cousin he was still a bachelor, and took Rab along just to help spend the necessary fiver. If they split it at two-pounds-ten apiece, how shall I, who bought no more than a lavender-bag, blame them? In any event, it was then, on the occasion I have described, that Robert Guthrie set eyes on Cecilia strolling about with her stolen badge of honour, and was completely bowled over.

The most I can say for *his* physical appearance is that he had very direct (though small) grey eyes and a good stuggy build. He was more than a few inches shorter than Cecilia, and more than a few years older; he was actually fifty. He was also one of the highest-salaried men in America, owing to some breakthrough he'd made in the field of industrial chemistry. —Here I rely on later information from our own, local Guthrie, who sometimes added it had been just a toss-up whether he himself, at Edinburgh, took Veterinary/Agriculture rather than Science. There is always a natural rivalry between cousins. Was it my favourite novelist Henry James who pronounced that in Boston it could amount to internecine warfare? He referred of course to the Boston in America, not our own Boston in Lincolnshire; East Anglia, after so much banging to-and-fro with the Danes, has settled into a generally rather tolerant community. Even the Dutch who came to teach us to drain, and then some of them to settle, were so tolerated and absorbed, the next biggest farm after Leys is still called Hollanders.

I happened myself to witness the moment of Cecilia's and Rab's first encounter. I had arrived late, from motives of economy, and Cecilia was still telling me the tale of her bouquet when the two Guthries (equally late, though let us hope not for the same reason), hove in view. Tam and I are old acquaintances; naturally he introduced his cousin at once, then to Cecilia beside me. For some reason Tam had never much liked Cecilia — otherwise the carnations might have been hers by right! — but as for Rab, he had plainly but to look to love.

I had twice in my life witnessed such a *coup de foudre* before: once at a bus stop in Saxmundham, when a young girl of very moderate attractiveness, and a youth definitely oafish, after eying each other for five minutes got on the bus with hands already entwined; the other at our local fish-and-chip shop (whose kind proprietress Mrs. Cook lets me take a fillet of plaice home wet), as a lorry driver set eyes on young Ellen behind the counter. Paying my ninepence, I felt a sudden positive charge of amorous electricity in the air — Cupid's arrow, so to speak, ricocheting off my own lean bosom — and though Ellen tossed her head and looked lofty, I had to tell her twice what the right change from half-a-crown was.

They are now married, with five or six children. —"Those lorry drivers, there's no holding them!" Mrs. Cook once observed to me; though from what other experience I cannot guess. Her husband Arthur was on a trawler.

Of course Robert Guthrie was a different kettle of fish altogether, but I recognized the same sudden electricity in the air — in fact, the *coup de foudre*.

7

(Men far less than women, I think, consciously look for love; it takes them by surprise, like a tile blown off a roof.) Equally of course Cecilia neither curled her fingers in his nor bridled and tossed her head, and Rab merely offered us refreshments in the marquee.

One always expects to be robbed at Fêtes — my lavender-bag at a shilling was flat as an April pease-cod — but the half-crown teas in the marquee I can only describe as bare-faced. By this time even the rock cakes were gone. However one was able to sit down. —A few minutes after we did so, up sidled a little girl sniffling.

"If you're lost," said I — I hope kindly, but even the tea was cold — "go and wait by the entrance till you're found."

Children are always getting lost at Fêtes, just as their elders are robbed; but this particular child's predicament turned out to be less usual and more sophisticated.

"I gave the flowers wrong," she stated dismally. "Mum's bin on at me ever since."

Her mother being Lady A.'s housekeeper, I could well believe it. Why I hadn't recognized Mabel sooner was due to her unusual finery of starched muslin and pink sash. I commonly saw her in darned jerseys.

"She says to get 'em back," continued Mabel, "an' have another go."

The hint, or plea, was obviously directed at Cecilia; only she and I had any idea what the child was talking about, and beyond the open side of the marquee could indeed glimpse Lady A. still on duty chatting to a stall-holder. Only where was the bouquet? Discarded under our tea-table. I stooped and fished it up and replaced it in Cecilia's hands, who I must say appreciated the whole situation with great swiftness.

"So you want my flowers back to give to someone else?" she asked gently. "Then you shall have them!" — and Mabel got not only the carnations but a kiss as well. It must have seemed like a kiss from a Fairy Godmother, the child's eyes so widened; but she couldn't have looked more bewitched than Rab Guthrie.

Lady A. I thought acted very well too, suddenly offered at half-past five the tribute she'd been there to receive on the dot of three, also now somewhat be-draggled. That is, she accepted it. So Mabel went home forgiven, and Rab back to Leys Farm under the spell of beauty matched by kindness.

3

It was of necessity a whirlwind courtship, since he was far too important and hard-worked to be able to extend his fortnight's visit by more than a week; but luckily he'd seen Cecilia at the Fête the very day after arriv-ing, and a village is almost as good as a cruise ship for throwing people together; one can't walk to the Post Office to buy a stamp without an encounter at every step; moreover Cecilia had the advantage — also enjoyed, I have noticed, by librarians and girls at cash-desks — of being always, so to speak, *there*. Of course if she'd kept a stationer's rather than a dress shop Rab's amorous path would have been even smoother: there was absolutely nothing he could buy from a ladies' dress shop; but he could still rely on its closing and liberating her from one till two, when if she happened to lunch out instead of upstairs, and if Rab happened to pass by as she emerged, what more natural than that they should pick up a sandwich together at the Copper Kettle? —And this apart from coffee breaks at eleven, during one of which I recall Lady A. rapping like an infuriated woodpecker for a turned-up hem. Before the first week ended Cecilia's coffee break and lunch hour had practically merged, and during the second Rab was regularly driving her out to dinner besides at one of the nice country inns in which our district happily abounds. (The Mariners' Arms for lobster, the Crown and Sceptre for duck.) Our own guest-house, Woolmers, has quite a reputation for home-made pâté and fresh vegetables, but was of course too near at hand to be driven to, and the car Rab hired in London was a Daimler.

I cannot say the village awaited the issue with bated breath, because there never seemed any doubt about it; unsurprised, no one blamed Cecilia in the least for getting married by special license even before she wore an engagement ring.

What chiefly surprised myself was the rapidity with which she was able to sell her shop. It was quite some time before I learned through our local estate agent that she'd been negotiating for several months with her successor Miss Wilson, who henceforward provided us with a very nice line in raincoats.

So in 1933 Rab Guthrie took Cecilia back to New York with him, where she became, one heard tell, quite a leader of fashion; also bore him the daughter she now on that cool but not cold, showery but not rainy, autumn-scented April day some twelve years later came back to collect.

4

Obviously I must explain how it happened that for the last five of those years Cecilia's daughter Antoinette was living under my roof.

Cecilia had returned once before, but literally by accident: in the June of '39 Tam Guthrie fell off a tractor and broke his ribs. What to a younger man would have been no more than a painful mishap resulted for Tam in complications leading first to pneumonia and eventually to his death. (After sixty a fall of any sort is to be avoided, which is why I put away my bicycle — or rather gave it away, to the Scouts, who I fear had to dispose of it as scrap iron.) There was nothing surprising about Tam's end, nor, essentially, about the way he left his property: all to be sold and merged in a trust fund to provide bursaries at his old university. What surprised us was that Rab came to the funeral. I have remarked earlier on the strength of Scottish-American family feeling, and of course he was a wealthy man: however, it then turned out that he and Cecilia were Europe-bound in any case, on a quite extended tour; their original plan (before Tam fell off the tractor) had been to disembark at Cherbourg. Now instead (Tam's obsequies fitting in so handily), they left ship at Southampton and put up for a couple of nights at Woolmers instead of the Crillon.

As Mrs. Brewer (my help, and a connoisseur of funerals) observed, they made all the difference. Without them the verger would scarcely have known whom to put in the front pew; the only other relative present was a lanky, sandy-haired young woman wearing a black armband, whom he'd put in the pew across the aisle, where she looked so solitary I took it upon myself to go and sit beside her. She appeared glad of countenance, also eager to explain her conspicuous place; she was Janet Guthrie, she told me, a second cousin; adding a moment or two later that though she honestly scarcely remembered Tam he'd put her through Veterinary College. As at a wedding before the arrival of the bride so at a funeral before the coffin is borne in there is always a little time for chat! —I was most interested, as I always am by any instance of a woman invading traditionally male territory, and in return told her who I was and where I lived, and invited her to come in and see me — an invitation I would have repeated after the service, only while I was having a word with Cecilia, she disappeared.

Cecilia, unlike Rab, was in tears. I didn't wonder; the language of the Church of England burial service is as beautiful and emotive as any chorus-ending from

Euripides. However often one hears it, and of course as one grows older one hears it increasingly often, it never loses impact. I must admit that even a chorus-ending of Euripides' I knew only by hearsay, as glossed in the note to a poem by Robert Browning; the phrase entering my mind, however, even as I pressed Cecilia's hand determined me to attempt to learn Greek ere too late. My father had been quite a scholar in Greek, and I still had all his books.

Though it was now July, I remember that morning as so unnaturally cold we all wore our darker, winterish garments quite gratefully. (One never puts one's heaviest coat into winter mothballs, in East Anglia!) However the morning after — (never a dull moment, in East Anglia!) — when the Guthries paid me a visit, the french windows of my sitting-room stood open to catch a breeze.

5

They brought Antoinette with them, as they'd brought her with them from New York; which Cecilia at least already recognized to have been an error.

"Such an infant, to be toted from Paris to Rome to Salzburg!" regretted Cecilia. "She's looking peaked already! Didn't I tell you, darling, we should have left her behind?"

"Yes," said Rab.

I did not recall him as being especially taciturn, but now he was properly, Scottishly dour. I liked him though for the way he held the baby so firmly and protectively on his knee. —When I say baby, remember that Antoinette was three. Yet she still seemed just a baby — possibly because she wouldn't say a word. She was perfectly well-grown, even sturdy. Her face was rather plain — a Dutch little face, I thought, round and unanimated, with a small mouth and her father's small grey eyes. There was nothing of Cecilia about her except her extreme fairness — but whereas Cecilia had locks the colour of honey, Antoinette's were just the colour of straw, and her eyebrows and lashes practically invisible. Probably most people would have considered Antoinette plain, except those who like myself have a fondness for the lint-headed, serious little creatures one sees in old Dutch paintings. I could easily picture that solemn small countenance intent above a bowl of eggs, or basket of oranges, responsible for their safe conveyance across a scrupulously clean red-tiled floor!

There were no such tiles underfoot at the moment. My sitting-room carpet is a rather nice old Aubusson, off which, before her father scooped her up, Antoinette had been trying to pick the roses. Now she wriggled down again, and towards myself; I held out a hand, and she instantly bit it — not to hurt, but as it were experimentally, as if to test (she a young rabbit) whether I were some kind of lettuce. Cecilia naturally scolded and apologized — but what are baby-teeth to the thumb of a hardened gardener? — and I felt Antoinette not at all unreasonable in objecting to apologize herself.

"Say sorry, darling!" bade Cecilia. "Tony, say sorry at once!"

But quite evidently Tony wasn't going to. Her small pink mouth remained obstinately shut.

"You mean you're going to let Mummy say it *for* you?" reproached Cecilia.

Which seemed perfectly acceptable to Antoinette, who after a second tentative nibble appeared to recognize something tougher than green-stuff, yet not inimical, and philosophically squatted down on my shoes.

"She's so shy, if there's a stranger she simply won't utter," explained Cecilia. "But you're certainly favoured!"

—I shall never forget how lovely she looked at that moment, bending forward from where she sat, her eyes on her little daughter, one hand stretched out, as if in an arrested caress, toward the smooth, lint-coloured head. In the six years since she left us Cecilia had grown even slenderer, but without the least angularity. There was a wonderful grace about her even more attractive than her beauties of hair and skin and feature — though these too seemed to me enhanced, as if by special cherishing. I could easily imagine her becoming a leader of fashion and a pride to her husband in New York! But even while Antoinette was still trying to undo my shoelaces (she didn't succeed), Cecilia's expression of maternal affection altered to an equally maternal expression of irritation — though directed rather towards her husband.

"When we left, she was quite rosy!" harked back Cecilia. "Now she's white as an egg! Didn't I tell you, darling, we should have left her with Miss Swanson? —Swedish," she added, in a hasty parenthesis to myself, "with absolutely every qualification!"

"Maybe I was wrong," said Rab quietly.

"You certainly were!" snapped Cecilia. "And there's still Paris and Rome and Salzburg ahead!"

It is always embarrassing to witness a tiff between husband and wife; I so to speak absented myself by lifting Antoinette up and letting her bite my thumb more conveniently from my lap. I only hoped Cecilia might not feel jealous, at such trust in as she said a stranger; but not at all. On the contrary —

"Actually I've suddenly had the most brilliant idea!" declared Cecilia, turning from her husband to myself with a lightened brow. "If we could only leave Tony with you, just for the month, and pick her up on the way home, I'm sure it would be far, far better for her!"

Extraordinarily enough I paused only a moment before agreeing: to look enquiringly at Rab. He for his part gave me as searching a look back; then with equal consideration contemplated my sitting-room, and the windows open to the garden, and the garden beyond. I suppose it all presented a picture of modest comfort and respectability, also of course he'd met me before.

"It might be a good idea at that," said he.

So it was arranged, after singularly little more discussion (I having lost my heart to Antoinette already), that while the Guthries toured Europe their daughter should be left in my care, and her parents brought her to deposit with me next morning, together with her clothes in a suitcase and a traveling-bag of toys.

The interim parting was remarkably painless. —I had taken the precaution of borrowing a basketful of tabby kittens with which to distract and console an infant in tears: Antoinette was obviously taken by them, she purred back like a kitten herself, but had not been crying. Cecilia quite rightly behaved as casually as possible; she and I equally, I think, reprobated Rab's too prolonged, too serious embracement of his small daughter before he finally released her and followed Cecilia out to the car.

Antoinette appeared to forget them instantaneously. Of course she had the kits to divert her, and then a glass of milk and bread-and-honey, before being tucked up for a nap in the cot I'd borrowed from the Women's Institute and had set up beside my bed. She seemed so cozy and content (and tired out, poor infant), I in fact gave her her boiled egg for supper there too; but still through the night lay with one ear alert in case she woke crying and needing comfort.

It was I who didn't sleep; not Antoinette.

When in the morning I got her up, and told her who Mrs. Brewer was, and showed her where the garden she could play in was, Antoinette accepted all in the same peaceable silence. I knew she wasn't mute — though now I came to consider it, I'd never heard her speak a word — because of her murmurings to the cats; but during those very first days of our life together it became clear to me that Cecilia's daughter was what in earlier times would have been called an innocent.

2

I have spoken of her, describing our first encounter, as a baby. Antoinette was in fact three. At three, she should have been able to untie my shoelaces quite easily. She should have not only uttered, but prattled. At three, Antoinette had still no more vocabulary than — a baby.

She was also as physically clumsy as a baby. If I had visualized her carrying bowl of eggs, basket of oranges, with serious, safe care, I soon discovered my error. Anything Antoinette was given to carry she dropped. It was as though her powers of concentration had an unusually limited span. She spilled even a cup of milk before she drank from it, and a spoonful of porridge before it reached her mouth — which of course made for a certain messiness that I had to discipline myself to accept without snapping, since one of the first things I learned about Antoinette was that she needed to be spoken to always very quietly, not to frighten her. It was specially important not to frighten her, not only for her own sake but because when frightened she was sick. I do not mean ailed: threw up. So I kept a supply of paper napkins always handy.

Other things that frightened her were strangers, blancmange, and dark glasses (especially if put on and off) but nothing so much as a voice raised in anger. I myself share the same distaste, though not of course to the extent of hiding under my bed; but on the rare occasions when Mrs. Brewer and her daughter-in-law "had words" in the kitchen, it was refuged under her cot that I discovered the suddenly missing Antoinette. Fortunately such incidents were rare, not only in my own quiet household but in the village generally, of which the motto, in the unlikely event of its ever attaining a coat of arms, might well be *De gustibus non est disputandum* — Anglicé, I don't blame you. Thus when two couples openly exchanged spouses without benefit of the Divorce Court, no one blamed them, no more than old Mrs. Bragg, supporting fifteen cats on her pension, was blamed for regularly each Sunday stealing all milk bottles left outside doors on her way home from Early Communion. Of old Mr. Pyke at Hollanders, so heavy-handed with a strap, woe betide any urchin caught scrumping in his orchard, it was remembered in excuse how he'd been thrashed as a boy, after his mother died, by a father even heavier-handed still. (What myself was to be excused for remains to be seen.) Then there was Major Cochran, ex–Royal Artillery, D.S.O. and bar, a positive menace each Armistice Day. Like every other, our village was only too willing to commemorate it, as a nice turnout for Old Comrades and the Boy Scouts and the St. John's Ambulance Brigade; owing to trouble with his dentures the Major's perennial recitation of *They shall not grow old* often held the band up marking time for as much as ten minutes; but no one blamed him . . .

So certainly no one in the village blamed Antoinette for being an innocent.

2

Spoken to always quietly and slowly, Antoinette understood perfectly. All that was needed was patience. She liked hearing poetry, if it had a strong rhythm, as in the *Lays of Ancient Rome*. I also introduced her — a rather abrupt declension, I fear! — to such easy nursery rhymes as *"Pussy-cat, pussy-cat, where have you been?"* — still substituting for the rather awkward monosyllable "queen" an easier disyllable: *"I've been up to London to buy a tureen."* Antoinette knew what a tureen was, because it was what I served our soup from. She also appeared to like the word for itself, for its soothing, crooning sound. ("Tureen, tureen!" I once heard her cajole a hedgehog.) Obviously she made no connection between sound and content; another word she liked was "vermin," overheard during an argument with my gardener on the subject of mole-traps. And indeed, for sound, what word is prettier —

the soft opening *v* that begins also violets, and velvet, and voluptuousness, then the tender dying fall that concludes? "Vermin" became in fact Antoinette's term of affection, applied alike to a cat, a dead toad, or myself.

I cannot describe what an affectionate little creature she was. If I say "creature" as I might say "animal," I too was accepting her innocence. Though childless, indeed unmarried, I have had ample opportunity (as in a village who has not?) to observe children from infancy onwards, and as a consequence believe firmly in the doctrine of original sin. The merest babe is covetous; a toddler no sooner finds its feet than employs them to trample its neighbour's mud-pie landmark; even the more sophisticated vices, such as exclusiveness, or cold-shouldering, bud early. (The exchange, "Can I play with you?" "No, you can't!" already adumbrating a Golf Club Committee faced by Jew or tradesman.) Antoinette cold-shouldered nobody — that is, who wasn't a stranger; and nothing in nature was alien to her.

The butcher's boy, for example, so glaringly cross-eyed he couldn't get a girl to go to the pictures with him, had in Antoinette almost an admirer. She seemed to find his squint an interesting variation from the usual — which when I remembered her dislike of dark glasses (also a facial variant), at first surprised me. But Kevin's squint came by nature; or possibly Antoinette thought he squinted deliberately, to amuse? In any case she never showed the least repulsion, unlike the girls who wouldn't go to the pictures with him, and more than once I found myself having to turn away joints of meat I hadn't ordered. —"If he waited for an order, we shouldn't see him more than once a week," pointed out Mrs. Brewer sensibly; and added that latterly he'd quite perked up.

No more did Antoinette cold-shoulder Mrs. Bragg who stole the Sunday milk. As I have said, no one blamed Mrs. Bragg (except her victims) though I personally felt she should either have made ends meet on her pension or else kept fewer cats. But she so smelled of her cats, even a whiff of her coat in the High Street made me hurry on — unless Antoinette were with me; Antoinette snuffed up the odour — natural to cats if not to Mrs. Bragg — rather appreciatively, and even lingered, thus giving the old thief the opportunity to touch me for a shilling. It was I who had finally to cold-shoulder Mrs. Bragg, my purse being quite unequal to support fifteen cats most of which ought to have been put down.

The village accepted Antoinette as kindly and sensibly as possible. If I took her shopping with me, she never encountered a look that wasn't good-tempered. She was still happiest in the garden, where we came to spend more and more of our time quite content without other company. Not that she was always at my side: she appeared to have a positive need for periods of solitude — it would seem absurd to say for meditation: but often for an hour at a stretch Antoinette would squat by herself under my artichokes, where soon her regular frequentation scooped out a little nest, like a down-to-earth squirrel's dray, between the strong protective stems . . .

3

I often wondered what kind of a life she could have led in New York. None of the beautiful toys left behind for her — and I have never seen prettier: a little lamb woolly in cashmere, a Japanese mousmé exquisite in silk, another doll dressed as a Puritan maid freshly disembarked from the Mayflower — engaged Antoinette's attention in the least. What she preferred for playthings were much more natural objects, as soon as she learned to find them in the garden, as toads, whether alive or dead.

I have always myself rather patronized toads — at least have never persecuted them. For the ugly beast that bears a precious jewel in its head I have great sympathy — that is, alive and hopping. Antoinette loved them dead as well, or even better, as more tolerant of being carried in a pocket. I so learned to accept this, it was only at the point of absolute decay and stench that I turned Antoinette's pockets out and put her smock to soak in disinfectant. Of course I always scrubbed her hands before meals.

In the parcel of toys she brought were also simple games, such as ludo and tiddlywinks, furnished with bright-coloured ivorine counters. What Antoinette offered in addition, and obviously preferred, were neat brown rabbit-droppings — actually the first signal to myself that I had rabbits in my garden at all. Of course the upper part (that I call my ambulatory) abuts on the heath; but I had never before realized — Antoinette never strayed beyond the garden's limit — how free they made of my whole domain.

Tiddlywinks, played with rabbit-droppings instead of ivorine counters, is naturally a slower game, in fact not the same game at all, but suited Antoinette all the better, who needed in everything to go slowly.

Turds deposited by stray dogs, if I happened to have left the gate open, were another matter. Though I could understand her appreciation of their almost cigar-like shapeliness and firm consistency, I never entirely reconciled myself to finding them cached under her cot. No more could Mrs. Brewer, and one or other of us regularly swept them out. Antoinette never looked for them again, but appeared to forget all about them as easily as she'd forgotten her parents.

Which obviously no normal child would have done; only Antoinette wasn't normal. She was an innocent.

I wondered very much, even more than I wondered about her life in New York, whether her parents knew. It seemed impossible they should not; yet nothing in their manner, during the short time we were in contact, suggested it — and parents are notoriously often the last to suspect, still less admit, any deficiency in their offspring. Either they are blinded by natural affection, or it is a species of insult to themselves which they instinctively reject. (How long, for instance, before Mrs.

Parrish, Mrs. Brewer's second cousin, was brought to admit her epileptic Bobby more than highly strung!) But then I remembered Cecilia's reference to Miss Swanson: "absolutely qualified" surely suggested more than an ordinary nursery-nurse? — and as a corollary that the Guthries already recognized their daughter's especial needs? In one way it was none of my business, my own, limited responsibility being to keep her safe and well and happy for a period of four weeks, which I had no doubt I could do quite easily; yet in another way (Antoinette's whole future so involved), it obviously was; and I painfully came to the conclusion that when at the end of the month her parents returned, it would be my duty to have a very plain talk with them.

I so flinched from the prospect, it sometimes kept me awake at night; worse, it sometimes kept Antoinette awake in her cot beside my bed. As I have said, she was extraordinarily sensitive to any sort of thunder in the air; after that first night of complete exhaustion, if I was restless, so was she. However I diverted my mind by mentally repeating Keats' odes to a Nightingale, Autumn, and a Grecian Urn — the tricky bit in the latter after *More happy love!/More happy, happy love!* needing such particular concentration as to exclude all other thoughts whatever. As it turned out, I need not have distressed myself — at least not so soon.

4

The outbreak of war, presaged as in 1914 by splendid weather (and I should very much like to hear a meteorologist's gloss on the point), caught the Guthries in of all places Salzburg, whence Rab, so important an industrial chemist, was I gathered practically shanghaied back to the States in his company's private plane. Cecilia naturally went with him — and who can blame her? As she wrote afterwards in one of her amusing letters, let alone her duty to her husband, how could she possibly face hostilities in a dirndl? Thus between Antoinette and her parents stretched an ocean suddenly so perilous, Cecilia absolutely refused to contemplate any immediate reunion.

Actually some hundreds of British children were to make the transit without disaster. (Our own policeman's Lenny had the time of his life in Brooklyn.) But in a succession of agitated cables Cecilia begged me to keep Antoinette safe where she'd been left, and I was more than willing to accept the charge, having come to love the child so dearly.

5

I do not love easily. Contrary to local belief, I am not in the least sweet-natured. I am highly critical, and easily displeased by circumstances which I unfortunately cannot control. It would accord better with my temperament, I often think, had I been born a fishwife, licensed to strong language and even physical belligerence; or else a tycoon with a retinue of understrappers, who when I said "come" or "go" came or went unquestioningly as helots. Being instead an elderly single woman of no position and small means, I do the best I can for myself by appearing sweet. —When I say, "no position," that is not entirely true: my late father was Vicar of the parish, and so long as I stay where I am I enjoy a certain status; but it is my reputation for sweetness that enables me to exert my will. If I say to Mrs. Brewer "come," even though she has rheumatism she cometh; or if to the window-cleaner "go, I'm lying down," off he goeth like a shot and comes back next day. Of course to preserve this fictitious character I need to do more than my share of disagreeables, such as watching by sickbeds till the doctor comes, at a pinch watching by corpses after he has left, breaking news of bereavements, and in general continuing to act as I'd acted all through my girlhood and then young-womanhood as an unpaid auxiliary curate. Early training stands me in good stead! I am nevertheless by nature far more fishwife or tycoon — who in the way of lack of inhibitions must have much in common — and have never doubted that at any real crisis I would react as ruthlessly as either, only so far there had been no occasion.

6

I made no attempt to explain this new development to Antoinette. She appeared, as I say, to have forgotten her parents completely: I should have had to begin by reminding her of them, which I felt quite beyond my powers. Antoinette lived in the present; in which she lived with me. To try and explain that she was not, immediately, going to live anywhere else seemed pure waste of time.

One result of the war was of course that all we civilians were named and numbered, and issued with identity and ration cards, and generally ordered about in a way which I personally found extremely irritating, but upon which I shall not dwell. I hope I am quite sufficiently patriotic, but I saw no point, nor do I now, in the nuisance of putting up blackout curtains along a coastline so inevitably defined by the North Sea, of which the German Admiralty presumably had maps. However there was a general interferingness abroad; Doctor Alice, for example, visited me quite unsummoned to check that my bronchitis was no worse than usual.

I have nothing against Alice Philpot — B.Sc., M.D.Lond. No one had. In East Anglia, the tradition of Elizabeth Garrett Anderson is still so living, there was no local prejudice against her (because she wasn't a man), whatever. Local farmers not only sent a hind to her for antitetanus inoculation as confidently as they took a dog to the local vet, but trusted her equally with a wife's birthing. To say I have nothing against Alice Philpot is in fact an understatement. I have the greatest respect for her, but I wish she would leave my lungs alone. I have had slight bronchitis, off and on, ever since I was a child, when no more notice was taken of it than to keep me out of the water, so that I have never learned to swim. Doctor Alice, however, with direful warnings against pleurisy, insisted on running her stethoscope over me several times a winter. It being now high summer, I felt entirely justified in refusing to strip to my vest and draw deep breaths. In fact I kept our conversation as short as possible, and for another reason besides my natural annoyance: I was reluctant for her to encounter Antoinette. The village accepted my child as an innocent, and didn't blame her and was kind to her; I had no doubt of Doctor Alice's kindness, but still apprehended her constitutional inability to let well alone.

Fortunately she cornered me within doors — actually at my desk casting up the month's accounts — and Antoinette was as usual in the garden. However just as Doctor Alice was about to leave, in the child wandered looking for me with in one hand a dead frog and in the other, I was sorry to see, a turd. —Doctor Alice paused.

"Isn't that the Guthrie child?" she asked interestedly.

"Yes," said I. "Antoinette. —Say good-morning to

Doctor Philpot, Antoinette," I added. "Or must I say it for you?"

It struck me even as I spoke that I was covering up for the child just as Cecilia had once covered up for her to myself; and only hoped Doctor Alice would be as easily bamboozled.

Antoinette for her part naturally took no notice of the injunction, but pridefully exhibited the turd.

"And go and throw that horrid thing away at once," said I, "and go and wash your hands . . ."

This again was for the benefit of Doctor Alice. I had no hope of Antoinette's obeying. It was a much longer sentence than I usually employed with her, also my tone of reprobation, towards such familiar treasure-trove, naturally surprised and dismayed. Antoinette simply looked dumber than usual.

"How old?" asked Doctor Alice pleasantly.

I said three.

"One doesn't see her about much," remarked Doctor Alice.

"She likes to stay and play in the garden," I glossed. "Don't you think she looks very well on it?"

"Very," agreed Doctor Alice — at which moment (and this I should have expected), Antoinette was sick. Luckily I had only to reach under the nearest cushion for a paper napkin, and cleaned her up in a matter of moments, at the same time juggling away into my handkerchief both frog and turd. Thus bereft, Antoinette was naturally sick again, but only a couple more napkins sufficed, after which she squatted quite contentedly on my shoes.

"You'll forgive me if I don't come to the gate with you?" said I.

"All young animals throw up," observed Doctor Alice. "Just let me know if she stops eating . . ."

7

Antoinette's appetite however even improved — partly perhaps through being so much in the open air. Of course I always put her to bed in the afternoon — too much sun makes a child fretty — whilst I myself took a nap in the cool of my sitting-room. Otherwise, the weather continuing so fine, we lived mostly in the garden, even to the extent of Antoinette's eating her bread-and-honey supper there — she rather welcoming the attentions of wasps and bumblebees, and I must say was never stung.

It was a happy time. I even felt a certain guilt, to be so happy; for all this while the wind of war was blowing. But even while the tempest shakes, almost blasts, the oak, the insects in its roots no doubt live out their lives much as usual, and the full gale never reached us. We were not bombed; from so agricultural a community not even all younger men were called up, and though of those who were, or who volunteered, some never returned, it was nothing like the deathly reap-and-bind of the First World War. (The 1914–18 Roll of Honour in our church had seventeen names inscribed on it; in 1945 — again I look ahead — there were only eight to add.) A major loss was of Doctor Philpot, who as soon as the bombing of London began returned to the hospital where she'd qualified. All thoroughly understood and respected her motives; we had always known ourselves remarkably fortunate to have so good a doctor in so small a community (though as I have said, her practice extended far beyond its bounds), and London's need was obviously immeasurably greater; but she was much missed.

It was a happy time. As I sat in the garden knitting or slicing beans, aware of Antoinette never farther off than under the artichokes or up in the thicket of saplings that bordered a high grassy walk, I found myself repeating again and again another line of Keats': *warm days will never cease . . .*

Then I received a letter from a Mr. Hancock, from an address in Gray's Inn, heralding a visit to discuss the future of Antoinette Guthrie, temporarily in my charge.

3

For a person who has lived to be sixty I have had remarkably little to do with lawyers. My father left the Bank his executors, and successive managers have always told me what to do. What I was originally advised, or told, to do was to buy an annuity: which still in mourning I did; and though in subsequent, more tycoonish frames of mind I often regretted it, at least I have never faced bankruptcy or being hammered at Lloyd's. Once indeed I determined to employ Counsel in defense of Mrs. Brewer's allotment encroached upon by the extension to the churchyard, but she weakly settled out of court.

I at least knew Mr. Hancock by repute, he having so efficiently wound up Tam Guthrie's estate; also as even lawyers were children once — as my favourite statue in all London, in Lincoln's Inn, reminds — so a solicitor is still a man; and most men enjoy a good tea.

Thus I made ready for Mr. Hancock new-baked scones, honey and home-made jam, very thin cress sandwiches, and a rather special cherry-cake prematurely snapped up from the Women's Institute Bring-and-Buy in aid of the Red Cross.

I gave Antoinette her own tea early. Naturally Mr. Hancock would want to see her, but I feared her messiness with food might give a wrong impression of both of us. I was most anxious to impress Mr. Hancock favourably. I deliberately, in advance, subdued all the tycoonish or fishwife side of my nature which his letter had naturally aroused. I meant to present myself humble before superior masculine opinion. Unluckily, but a moment after he arrived, and we had mutually introduced ourselves, I heard myself quite sharply instructing him to keep his glasses either on or off. For they were sunglasses: Antoinette, at my heels at the gate, was already flinching, when he took them off, perhaps the better to look at her; as he absently put them on again I sensed her beginning to take fright, and all too well saw the probable consequences. I still regretted having spoken so sharply as I did; Mr. Hancock looked surprised, as well he might.

"Antoinette," I apologized, "doesn't like dark glasses put on and off. Let me give you a cup of tea."

Mr. Hancock said it would be welcome. —He had a very slight Scottish accent, just sufficient to remind me of Rab Guthrie's; Scots notoriously hanging together I wasn't surprised, quite apart from the connection with Tam. Antoinette instinctively kept to the garden;

Mr. Hancock (glasses now definitely off), followed myself indoors and to the tea-table. —It was once a curtsy dowagers recommended, to give a female time to think; in the present day and age I myself would recommend pouring tea.

I poured, Mr. Hancock drank. He also ate. The cress sandwiches he seemed to enjoy particularly, as recalling tennis-parties at the home of friends in Norfolk whose patronymic at least was familiar to me. We had really a pleasant chat. But the pause for reflection advantages both sexes equally, and I was all the time conscious of his shrewd lawyer's eye glancing over, taking in (just as Rab Guthrie's had done), every detail of my sitting-room, and through the french windows a lunar at the garden outside.

"And now —" said Mr. Hancock, putting down his cup.

"And now?" said I, refilling mine.

"I have a proposition to put to you," said Mr. Hancock, "which you may well reject at once, though I hope not. The child's parents —"

"Antoinette's," said I. —Little animals, however affectionate, may be anonymous, but children have names.

"Antoinette's parents, then," resumed Mr. Hancock, "having decided it too dangerous to send for her at the moment — indeed at any immediately foreseeable moment — some stable arrangement must obviously be made for her."

"Obviously," said I.

"Would you consider keeping her here with you for perhaps even a term of years?"

This was actually the first time, so suddenly had war struck us, that I contemplated its possible duration at all; to my shame (but then I had spent so many sleepless nights!), the phrase "a term of years" actually rejoiced me. Indeed I was willing, I assured Mr. Hancock, to keep Antoinette as long as necessary; and added, which seemed even more important, that I ventured to believe she would come to no harm.

Again Mr. Hancock took a good look round. He had a proper lawyer's eye! I was glad to remember my income tax, also rates paid, and my bank account not overdrawn.

"No; I can't see a bairn coming to harm here," said he thoughtfully.

Why I should have been less offended to hear Antoinette referred to as a bairn than a child I cannot explain — unless because Burns and Sir Walter between them have invested the whole Scots tongue with some insinuating glamour? Mr. Hancock's "bairn" was so kindly sounding, I began to like him. Of course I thought better of him too for his confidence and trust in me, which to my egoism proved him a good judge of character. But this very trustfulness, however flattering, at the same time roused my conscience; and I felt it absolutely indispensable to say, though I hadn't said it to Doctor Alice, that Antoinette wasn't quite like other children.

To my surprise, Mr. Hancock nodded.

"So her father suspected," said he. "Her mother I understand won't hear of it. But it was another reason why Guthrie agreed to her being left here originally; if I may say so, you made a very good impression on him."

I was naturally gratified and flattered afresh. My conscience, less venal, remained active.

"There is still the point," said I, "whether she shouldn't be receiving some sort of special treatment; though if I have to take her up to London for it, or even to Ipswich, I really couldn't answer for the consequences; so far, here, she hasn't been even on a bus. And she can say tureen."

"Tureen?" repeated Mr. Hancock, I suppose in not unnatural surprise.

"And vermin," I continued. "I don't pretend she means what you or I would mean, but she knows what *she* means. One just has to learn. All the same, it would relieve my mind if before you go you had a word with Doctor Alice — I mean Philpot."

Again the old needle-nose surprised me.

"In point of fact I took her in on my way," said he. "She and Robert Guthrie, you may recollect, being acquainted . . ."

I recollected no such thing, and said so.

"Maybe it was just a call he paid," offered Mr. Hancock. "Certainly he was able to give me the address, and she remembers him perfectly."

Of course, when I thought back, even within a couple of days there would have been ample opportunity. Perhaps, and this struck me as most likely, it was after, not before the plan to leave Antoinette with me that her father called on Doctor Alice; which in turn would explain the latter's visit to myself overtly to check my bronchitis. If there is one thing I abominate it is duplicity — yet I recognized an indirect approach to the child (which I now felt sure it had been), as both sensible and kind; I could well imagine Antoinette's terror under a stethoscope! All the same, no one enjoys having been bamboozled, and I waited for Mr. Hancock to continue in I hoped impolite silence.

"Her only prescription," he added, "is T.L.C."

It sounded like some new sort of drug. But I am not easily bamboozled twice. I scented an esoteric joke such as all professionals enjoy together to the bafflement of the laity; and again waited.

"Or tender love and care," glossed Mr. Hancock. "In short, like Antoinette's father, and now, I may say, like myself, she feels there can be no better circumstances. She diagnoses the child simply retarded, not autistic. The only question is whether you yourself are prepared to shoulder the burden."

I said I was.

"Then all that is left is to settle the financial aspect," said Mr. Hancock.

Upon which, to my amazement, he proceeded to explain that the Guthries reckoned Antoinette's keep and expenses at five pounds a week, that is — since he spoke of years — our organist's annual stipend. It was ridiculous, and I said so. Antoinette's extra cost to me couldn't amount to a fifth; also I am not a professional taker-in of lodgers. Mr. Hancock heard me out patiently but remained unmoved. As he said reasonably enough, he had his instructions: a cheque would in any case be paid quarterly into my account, to cash or not as I pleased.

"Or make a nest-egg of for her?" suggested Mr. Hancock.

Which was actually what I did. Of course I wasn't so stubborn as not to draw on it for so to speak extras, which is how Antoinette came to take riding lessons, of which more later.

4

So now we settled down, Antoinette and I, to live together for as long as the war lasted; and I had better describe the village that was our nutshell.

I say "village," though it is really almost large enough to rate as a small township, because the atmosphere is still a village's. The inhabitants are very proud of this, as making for a quiet life and good-neighbourliness, and often point it out not only to strangers but to each other. There are no remarkable features — even the most local of guidebooks, mere pamphlets privately printed, illustrated with amateur pencil sketches, do not mention us; but the High Street, if without special character, is agreeable for its human scale: no building higher than three storys except Woolmers, and that, being as broad as tall, doesn't so much dominate as watch comfortably over its lesser neighbours like a broody hen over chicks. Such big houses are usually found farther outside a village, but whatever rich wool-merchant originally built it — hence the name — must have liked to be more in the thick of things. Evidently the riches declined; Woolmers now, as I have described, being a guest-house. The only other building of any consequence is The Chantry, situated halfway up the hill to the church — by *its* name recalling some monkish establishment, or probably appanage : a semi-Palladian villa erected on such a patch of flat ground as might have been pasture. I never remembered its being occupied, but there was local rumour of a Nabob and musical parties. At present it is entirely derelict, its gates rusted on their hinges and the rose-beds beyond run to riot.

Even our church, in a country famous for churches, hasn't much to recommend it to a guidebook. It is neither thatched, like Theberton's, nor majestic, as at Lavenham, nor like Blythburgh's angel-roofed. No one ever came to take rubbings of its brasses, of which indeed there were but two, and neither particularly interesting — no knight in armour, no double file of kneeling sons and daughters, just brief commemorations on the north wall of two now completely forgotten worthies. The name of one was Brewer, but when I enquired of my own Mrs. Brewer she looked blank. There'd been Brewers around, said she, since time and time, but doubted an immediate kinship; and if any old auntie forgot (in the housewifely sense) to keep the brasses rubbed, Mrs. Brewer didn't blame her.

My own house stands a little way uphill from The

Chantry. Like much else in the village I can best describe it as pleasant but undistinguished. Its chief advantage is a sizable garden, which has the further advantage (owing to the rise) of being on two levels; affording me, above usual lawn and flower-beds, the narrow, grassy, sapling-fringed terrace I call my ambulatory. I grow no vegetables — I have too many kind neighbours with allotments — except artichokes, and those chiefly for their beauty. In my opinion there is no plant more majestically handsome. Even its earliest shoots rise in silver-grey promise of classic foliation; at full height, before blooming first into a brief edibility, then into enormous cobalt-blue thistle-heads, the overarching ribs are simply cathedral-like. Of course with so much ground I need to employ a gardener two days a week, but am happy to say he is not a character.

Our society is small. Major Cochran and Mr. Pyke I have mentioned; there is naturally a Vicar, and his wife, the Gibsons, whom I am more than happy to see in my old home; if I have never taken up their invitation to pop in and out just as usual it is by no means because I do not like them, but because I have had quite enough of my old home. The well-to-do people of the neighbourhood, though not native to it, are the Cockers, who bought Cross Hall some ten years ago. They are very public-spirited; it is to Arthur Cocker the church owes its new organ, while his wife, Beatrice, practically subsidized the Women's Institute bill for visiting lecturers — in fact the Women's Institute was lectured at until boredom set in, though here I must a little blame my old friend its secretary: however natural to make hay while the sun shone, I thought at the time, and still think today, that neither Romance Languages nor Early Mayan Art was a suitable topic.

But be fair to the Cockers! Nothing is easier than to write a cheque, if one has the means: when our £250 a year organist shot off to help man a barrage balloon, Beatrice Cocker actually played the organ, each Sunday. With the same kindness as shown by Mrs. Gibson, she pressed myself to slip in and play on it too whenever I liked; but I had had quite enough of playing voluntaries. (Even as a girl the term struck me as a misnomer: one didn't *volunteer* a voluntary, one was conscripted.) However, I dine with the Cockers I suppose twice a year, and they are so kind, they always offer to send their car for me; but I prefer to hire Alfred's taxi and keep my independence and leave early before bridge.

Ours was also, until the war, a very static society, unenlivened by any influx of summer yachtsmen as at Aldeburgh or Yarmouth or Felixstowe. It wasn't the sea our village neighboured but the mere branch of an estuary, by which no more than a dinghy-sailing club had established itself, with no more for clubhouse than a derelict bungalow. It struck me very much — (here again I look ahead) — how swiftly and efficiently our American allies of the U.S. Air Force took it over and put life into it. Suddenly scraped down, made weatherproof, fresh-painted, the bungalow looked like new even before a bar was installed; also within a matter of hours, or so it seemed to us slower-paced natives, inside the shingle-ridge they bulldozed out a quite sizable swimming pool. For the American commanding officer (one of the most charming men I ever met), had the sense to take local opinion on the danger of our estuary's swiftly turning and as swiftly running tide, and as he said (we thought rather wittily), would prefer to see his crews drowned off the French coast rather than the East Anglian. He also, with especial kindness, on Saturdays and Sundays, when any child had the pool's liberty, always put one of his men in charge — not only a great boon to all our small fry's parents, but an added attraction to the small fry themselves.

They had a wonderful time, at the American swimming pool. The only reason I never took Antoinette there was because I cannot swim — at the deep end it would have been I in danger of drowning — and I knew it but a child's-scramble across the shingle-ridge to the estuary itself. Perhaps I was overcautious; but a son of one of Mrs. Brewer's cousins, quite a strong swimmer, caught by the turning tide, had eventually been fished up unrecognizable save for the UP BOBBERS tattooed across his chest — the Bobbers being a local football club of which he was a great follower.

I have never cared for crabs, which is a pity, since they are so cheap. In general Antoinette and I subsisted on an almost vegetarian diet. It was also a rather monotonous diet, since above all she disliked any sort of change, resisting even tapioca instead of rice pud-

ding — (blancmange, as I have said, positively frightened her, possibly because its quivering suggested it
was alive?) — or chocolate in place of cocoa: as
though instinctively recognizing how narrow a path
she needed to keep her balance. Thus for breakfast
Antoinette never wanted anything but a boiled egg,
and for supper bread and honey, and at midday chicken
and salad, or when the weather grew colder chicken
broth. Since I couldn't be bothered to cook separately
for myself, it made, as I say, for monotony, but luckily
I am no more a connoisseur of food than I am of wine.

Indoors what Antoinette liked best was a huge old
leather steamer trunk, once the property of my Uncle
James in the Indian Civil Service. I was far from imagining it was the impasto of exotic labels — Delhi, Simla,
Ootacamund — that attracted her; she couldn't read;
to my mind she regarded it as some large benevolent
animal, mute as herself, like an elephant. She liked to
climb into and curl up in it. With some vague recollection of *The Mistletoe Bough* I had the big domed lid
taken off its hinges — which Antoinette then employed
to push herself about the floor in, like a coracle, and
we kept it for convenience in the embrasure behind my
dressing-table.

2

After the first bombs began to drop our little society
however increased, as elderly and retired Suffolk-born
homed to their native soil. Some found hospitality with

relations, others rented cottages; Woolmers boasted quite a star resident-guest in the person of a retired Admiral, Sir David Thorpe, whose son and daughter-in-law I remember depositing him there and then casting off with true naval celerity. As young Mrs. Thorpe nevertheless found time to explain, they felt he'd be happier by the sea. I have already described our situation as on no more than an estuary, but I didn't blame her. However expert in naval matters, Sir David was an uncommon old bore. But he was still almost handsome, in a traditionally beaky sort of way, and undoubtedly made as good an impression in Woolmers' dining-room as did his name on its register; moreover Mrs. Brewer's niece Jessie, who was housemaid there, reported him a very fair tipper.

So our little society increased, and not by addition of the elderly alone: several pregnant young wives, their husbands overseas, came to nest amongst us, and after vanishing into Ipswich Maternity for a week returned to push prams. I cannot say how much I admired the courage and prettiness of these young women. My own mother, as I was all too often reminded, after bearing my own skinny six-and-a-half pounds had to lie on her back for a month and be fed from a cup with a spout.

There also arrived a Cocker daughter-in-law with young family — her husband a Colonel, but who came on leave not from overseas but from the War Office; it was probably this circumstance that made her attempts to patronize our other young wives such a failure. In any case East Anglia's is a very democratic, libertarian climate. She improved however on acquaintance, and all three children took riding lessons, which was a great boon to Honoria Packett, and incidentally to Antoinette.

The center of Antoinette's personal world was still my garden, where she appeared to find inexhaustible interest. She appeared able to contemplate — she whose powers of attention had once so brief a span! — a nettle or a broken twig for half an hour at a time. Nothing in nature was worthless, or undelighting to her. —I must confess that this trait, however much I approved it, sometimes disconcerted me; as when she once produced for my admiration, unwrapped from a bit of newspaper, the huge, glaucous, redly striated jelly of a bullock's eye — gift of Kevin. But why should I feel such repulsion, when Antoinette obviously didn't? To her it was perhaps as beautiful as a Turner sunset. I did my best to regard it as such, mentally transferring it, flat, onto canvas. But alas my imagination failed, and I caused her to bury it under the artichokes without delay, on the pretext that it would spoil. I also, rather meanly, had a word with the butcher; but there were occasions when Antoinette's stomach was stronger than mine.

She had in fact almost stopped being sick at all. It was only when frightened that she threw up, and there was little now to alarm — I always careful to speak to her in a low, slow voice, and Mrs. Brewer having learned to do the same. I still kept a supply of paper napkins handy, in my shopping-bag and under cushions and so on, but came to need them less and less, as Antoinette slowly but surely developed from a small animal into a small child.

She not only learned to eat food without spilling it, and hold an egg without dropping it; given even a cup and saucer to carry, she became quite sure-handed. She was also accepting to be cleaner. Most children enjoy splashing in a bath: Antoinette, as though the accumulated smells of toad and turd and old Mrs. Bragg afforded her a sort of physical cushioning against a world still strange, and possibly inimical, at first needed to be put into a bath by (my own) superior force. But after some months she accepted to be bathed because it was something that happened to her every day. Anything that happened every day became in time familiar, and therefore acceptable, to Antoinette; and that she was no longer so smelly I must admit came as a relief, I having a rather sensitive nose.

Mrs. Brewer too appreciated the change. "Clean as a Christian!" declared Mrs. Brewer approvingly — which brings me to the matter of religion, with which as a Vicar's daughter I may have been expected to show more concern already. Mrs. Gibson undoubtedly thought me lax, and more than once promised that Antoinette, in toddlers' Sunday School, would never be asked questions. I refused the kind offer nonetheless, my child being so inapt to sit still anywhere indoors for more than five minutes. However I taught her the Lord's Prayer — that is, repeated it to her every night after she was in bed, and regularly to my own "Amen" Antoinette chimed in with "Vermin."

Obviously the syllables are much alike. "Amen," said I; "Vermin," said Antoinette; but I sometimes feared only from affectionateness.

3

The day before she left for London Doctor Alice came and almost humorously ran her stethoscope over me. Between deep breaths —

"And Antoinette?" said I, looking her in the eye.

"Just the usual treatment," said Doctor Alice blandly.

At which moment — as almost precisely a year earlier — in came Antoinette. Only now she didn't so much wander as stump. She joined us, that is, quite purposefully, and to Doctor Alice's pleasant "Hello" answered with an equally pleasant "Tureen." I confess I hoped she might have added "vermin" — but even tureen was such an advance on being sick, I was glad Doctor Alice heard it.

"She is, isn't she, making progress?" I asked.

"Yes," said Doctor Alice.

It was from a bottle of grocer's sherry that I poured her a stirrup-cup. I have never ceased to regret, however foolishly, not opening the last of my father's Pedro Domecq.

5

We were now medically under the overextended aegis of an elderly doctor who had retired to Walberswick to devote himself to fishing, and whose return to practice was no light contribution on his part to the war effort. Fortunately we are a very healthy community, with a good chemist and a fund of homely experience in the way of feeding colds and starving fevers. In fact I never saw the old boy but once, at the funeral of one of his patients who happened to be my cousin. Antoinette had measles when all the other children did, and kept in bed for a fortnight, like all the other children, like all the other children recovered.

Physically at least there was no doubt of her thriving. She outgrew her cot within a couple of years. (The Women's Institute offered a replacement, but Antoinette was so attached to her cot, the sight of its being dismantled was too distressing, so I simply let down the foot and made an extension from a nicely padded piano-seat.) In the big trunk, instead of being wadded with cushions, she soon fitted as snugly as an apple in its dumpling, lapped by no more than a blanket; and pushed herself about so vigorously in her coracle its lid, Mrs. Brewer more than once remarked we might as well be having the sweep in. I never attempted to make sense of Mrs. Brewer's observations. They were so to speak gnomic, in their reference to long but un-coordinated experience.

I cannot say Antoinette grew any prettier or more animated. Her smooth round face had normally only two expressions: of bland, catlike content when happy, and when put out, a lion-cubbish scowl. All she essentially needed, in the way of speech, was purr and snarl. So I took it for great encouragement when she said tureen to me.

It was a slow process, educating a little animal into humanity, but fortunately patience is my strong suit; and what was heartening was that every now and then, after weeks and months without any seeming progress at all, there would come sudden breakthroughs as when a plant almost given up for good suddenly puts forth a leaf. To anyone except myself I suppose they would have seemed minuscule indeed: one was when at the end of the Lord's Prayer Antoinette spontaneously said "Vermin" of her own accord, before prompted by my "Amen"; another when, left in the kitchen with a basket of peas, she of her own accord began shelling them. But on one point I had to admit complete failure. Of all things, I would wish to teach a child the love of reading, not to be exchanged, as Lord Macaulay so rightly observes, for all the wealth of India, and which must begin with *ABC;* but against any sort of literacy Antoinette's mind appeared completely closed.

The set of alphabet blocks I bought her, when she was five, she employed chiefly to set up shelters for hedgehogs — or so I judged the sort of laagers neatly arranged both under the artichokes and on the terrace above. I never actually observed Antoinette making these dispositions — like a little animal she could be very secret — but that was where I found her alphabet blocks, before weather decayed them into illiteracy.

In some ways she was also cunning as a little animal. She discovered all sorts of ways, for example, of getting back into the house, after I'd closed the sitting-room windows behind her; by back or front door, of course, but also through the shaft to my long-disused coal cellar, whence she suddenly emerged in the kitchen like a cheerful mole to give me a surprise. It was a variant of hide-and-seek I was only too glad to promote, since another thing I wanted Antoinette to learn (second only to reading) was to play games. Especially with other children. Playing with its co-evals is a child's natural introduction to social life; it learns in the first place to keep rules. Our village infantry would have accepted Antoinette willingly, if slightly *de haut en bas,* she being an innocent; the stumbling-block was her extreme antipathy to any sort of violence. Violence is implicit in children's games, from *"Who shall we send* to fetch him away?" to "Here comes a chopper to chop off your head." Even Ring-o'-roses, with its "All fall down," frightened Antoinette. Yet I felt it important that she should at least consort with other children, and felt riding lessons quite an inspiration.

<h1 style="text-align:center">2</h1>

Even before these started, however, there was another and quite important breakthrough. One morning when I returned from a solitary shopping round, what was my surprise to see Antoinette, whom any unfamiliar face had hitherto so alarmed, squatting peaceably in the garden with a total stranger.

Mrs. Brewer caught me at the gate to explain it was a Miss Guthrie, which was why. (I am used to Mrs. Brewer's shorthand way of speech: why the young woman had been allowed in to wait for me.) But what was a patronymic to Antoinette? I quite rejoiced that it meant nothing, and that of her own accord, and even in my absence, she had accepted a stranger as not necessarily menacing . . .

Janet Guthrie was of course not a complete stranger to myself. She was the young woman I'd sat beside at Tam's funeral, and I recognized her at once. Now she was taking a holiday in Suffolk, on foot, with a rucksack, rubbing brasses. It didn't surprise me. Obviously all Guthries — as indeed all Scots — were gluttons for education, so that even a holiday had to have its cultural aspect: a rucksack equating the traditional bag of oatmeal. However when I warned that our own church had no brasses of interest at all, she pleased me very much by saying she knew it, but had thought she'd pay me a call.

"I looked for you after the funeral," said I, "but you'd vanished."

"I saw you talking to the Rab Guthries," said Janet. "They're the rich Guthries, like Tam; we're the poor ones."

Since she seemed to regard this as sufficient and total explanation I didn't press the point — but what a complicated clannishness the words revealed! From her tone they might have fought on opposite sides at Flodden. I remembered also there'd been no mention of a Janet Guthrie in Tam's Will; still he'd put her through Veterinary College; so she came to his funeral . . .

All this time Antoinette sat cheerful and placid, actually upon, and digging her heels into, the rucksack; and as it suddenly occurred to me that she and our visitor were, however tenuously, blood-related, I identified her to Miss Guthrie as Rab and Cecilia's daughter Antoinette, and explained how it came about she was living with me in Suffolk.

"I hope I'm not making her shy?" said Janet. "So far she hasn't said a word."

Quite with an air of putting her oar in, "Vermin, tureen," pronounced Antoinette.

"Now you've heard her whole vocabulary," said I.

Janet took this with such calm, I wondered whether she'd perhaps known another child like Antoinette;

but if she had she didn't say so, and with good manners I appreciated let the matter rest.

Over the table — for of course I kept her to lunch — we had a most interesting conversation about her work as a vet, and the small house she'd found to live in just as independently as I did in mine, though even more quietly; for her practice was in the wilds of Caithness, where it was well to have bees to tell any news to, said Janet, if you wanted to keep the use of your tongue! But she was obviously flourishing there; admittedly with so many men away it had been comparatively easy to set up; and at first there'd been some slight anti-female prejudice. "But I wore it down!" said Janet cheerfully. "It took me a year or so, but I wore it down!" — and now she felt quite established.

I liked Janet Guthrie very much, and told her that whenever she was in Suffolk again she must come and have another meal with me. At that she suddenly cocked a sandy eyebrow and grinned.

"To be truthful, a meal was what I had in mind!" said she.

I didn't blame her, even, or because, she'd accounted for the best part of a boiling-fowl. I was still sorry when she went. —I particularly appreciated her behaviour over the incident of the rucksack. We had left it in the garden; Antoinette, allowed to get down before coffee, over which Janet and I chatted on a little, had emptied everything out and got inside herself. Janet Guthrie gently yet firmly (as she might have handled a young beast) hauled her out by the scruff and then patiently repacked a pair of pajamas, three or four pairs of socks, a textbook on diseases in cattle, a sponge-bag, a light mackintosh, a writing-pad and a first aid kit.

I was sorry to see her go, and even sorrier that she didn't come back; but let me proceed to Antoinette's riding lessons.

3

Our local riding stable is run by Honoria Packett, of whom personally I shall say little. I have never liked horsey women, and Honoria is moreover jocular — her loud Ha-ha! all too accurately imitating the sound of trumpets. But she managed her riding school very well, and even though it was now, owing to wartime restrictions, reduced to a string of children's ponies, they were reassuringly sturdy and well-shod. A further advantage was that with no adults' hacks at hire, she would now collect a child at its door, to be paced sedately on a leading-rein before gaining the open moorland or heath, and so came each Tuesday and Friday to collect Antoinette along with the three Cocker children.

I shall never forget my first sight of Antoinette on pony-back. It was a Shetland, the baby's mount. To begin with, such was her instant delight and affection she hugged it round the neck almost to the point of throttling; a pony being larger than a frog, she hugged it all the harder. Honoria detached her, I must say quite gently, and then lifted her into the saddle, and

57

set her feet in the stirrups, and led her on the leading-rein; so quietly, I, on foot, easily kept up with them past the church and then up onto the heath.

The young Cockers were all older than Antoinette, also more experienced. "Now trot!" ordered Honoria. Off the three tittupped in a wide, evidently familiar circle, not bunched together but keeping at a proper distance so that Honoria could scan them individually for backs straight and heels down. Evidently they passed muster, for after about ten minutes —

"Now canter!" called Honoria.

The change of rhythm was like that from a jig to a waltz, and achieved, at least to my own inexpert eye, quite beautifully. —But not so to Honoria's. "John, you're letting Mustard break!" she shouted, to the youngest Cocker. "Rein in and start again!" Alas, John reined in so abruptly he lost a stirrup, and as his siblings (I fear contemptuously) gave him a wide berth, Honoria instinctively abandoned Antoinette to trot up to him.

Whereupon Antoinette, or perhaps rather her pony, decided to canter too. As if bored by so much walking, and then standing, the little beast, with Antoinette on his back, neatly nipped into place behind the two elder Cockers, and cantered after.

Antoinette at least didn't fall off. She hung on, it must be admitted, at first by his mane. But the second time round it was to the saddle she clung, feet feeling for the stirrups. "All halt!" shouted Honoria, herself dismounting and running to catch Antoinette's bridle and lead her back. "Terribly sorry!" she panted, as soon as they were beside me. "It shouldn't have happened, and I'll see it won't happen again. But she's certain got guts, your little dumbo!" neighed Honoria.

I always found her offensive. Antoinette's riding lessons were nonetheless a success. In the first place she enjoyed them, and in the second she for the first time established a normal relationship with other children. It remained slight, the young Cockers just said "Hello" to her, but after the fourth or fifth lesson Antoinette was saying "Hello" back, which I felt an important addition to her vocabulary. The Shetland's name was Pepper, so Antoinette learned that too. There were now four words she could pronounce perfectly: vermin, tureen, pepper and hello.

And suddenly, months after Janet Guthrie's visit, she surprised me with the far more difficult vocable "rucksack"; so then there were five. I strung them together to make a proper sentence for her: *"Hello; in my rucksack I have vermin, pepper and a tureen,"* and Antoinette learned it off and repeated it apparently with all the pleasure I myself should have felt in being able to repeat a chorus-ending of Euripides, which as yet I could not. —None of the texts from my father's bookcase had been much use to me, requiring as they did a fair knowledge of Greek already. I had difficulty in even identifying a chorus-ending from Euripides on the page. However the next time I was in Ipswich I found a modest elementary handbook, and began from the beginning with my alpha-beta.

That the young Cockers for their part, though accepting and tolerating, never took much notice of her, was rather an advantage. As I have said, anything new needed to be taken very slowly, with Antoinette, and young Mrs. Cocker had no reason in the world to apologize to me for not inviting her to birthday-parties.

It was still a sign of Antoinette's difference from other children that she had no conception of a birthday. To most children, birthdays are of such cardinal importance, almost the first question one asks of another is how old are you? Antoinette was in fact now six, but perfectly unaware of it, and even I might have lost count but for the birthday presents arriving each year from New York — and then indeed, owing to the war, often months late.

4

Cecilia otherwise wrote punctually, describing how busy she was with Bundles for Britain — (she organized concerts and balls for them) — and always ending with a few lines for Antoinette, such as, *"My precious, your mummy misses you so much, she thinks of you all the time,"* which messages put me in something of a quandary. Though Antoinette couldn't read, I might have read them to her; she still wouldn't take in any meaning, having no conception of a mother. I was no usurper: Antoinette's relation to myself, I believed, and was happy to, was essentially that of a young rabbit to a lettuce — source of food, shelter, and general point of repair. In the end I simply suppressed the messages altogether.

But soon a worse quandary arose. *"Isn't it surely time Tony wrote a letter to me?"* complained Cecilia. *"Tell her she must be a good girl and mind her book, so she can write to her mummy!"*

Antoinette could no more write than she could read; but how to explain why — involving as it did the child's whole predicament — by letter? Not there to witness her daughter so obviously thriving, Cecilia must have been thrown into deep (and as I believed unnecessary) distress. She might have imagined a little idiot. So at last I decided to employ a subterfuge. I clasped Antoinette's fingers round a pencil, and guided them to trace in capitals DEAR MUMMY I HOPE YOU ARE WELL LOVE AND KISSES.

I had intended to make her sign, *Antoinette,* but though the ploy began as a game she soon tired of it, and was wriggling to get away at WELL. However Cecilia was apparently satisfied, for she didn't raise the point again.

Antoinette's father never wrote to her at all. He was obviously even busier than Cecilia, and I imagined better realized the inutility. I didn't blame him. In Mr. Hancock and Doctor Alice he had left the best agents he could to watch over his daughter's well-being under my roof. He couldn't know Doctor Alice departed for London — whence in fact she never returned; she lost her life in one of the last bombings.

So did Rab Guthrie lose his life in the war. In the

summer of '44 Cecilia had graver news to report than a row of seats unsold at a Bundles for Britain concert: that she was a widow, her poor darling Rab having literally worked himself to death. I could well believe it; he'd always struck me as a worker, and I had seen what pressure the war could put on just a pig-man, let alone an industrial chemist. In a way I quite mourned him — particularly because he'd never seen his daughter on a pony. Cecilia for her part (she wrote) felt such an appalling sense of loss, her only hope of avoiding a nervous breakdown was to throw herself more than ever wholeheartedly into Bundles for Britain; that is until the war ended, and she could at last seek her only possible true consolation by coming back to collect Antoinette. Though it might be difficult to get an air passage quite immediately, she had several useful connections.

Even at the moment of reading such sad news, the word "collect" struck me unfavourably; it is a parcel, some inanimate object, one collects, not a child. But perhaps I was oversensitive; and with Cecilia's postscript, *"Perhaps no need to tell Tony?"* I thoroughly agreed. If Antoinette had no conception of a mother, no more had she of a father; and one learns to mourn soon enough.

So I kept the news to myself.

In the meantime we enjoyed such another exceptional spell of fine weather, Antoinette grew brown as a berry as we lived day after day in the garden. The very sunniness seemed to call for extra treats: extra strawberries, for instance, extra staying-up-lates to see the moon rise. Even Mrs. Brewer was affected; I remember her once taking it upon herself, at midmorning, while I sat knitting and watching Antoinette, to bring me out a glass of sherry — she who had never handled the decanter before. "Go on, haven't you earned it?" said Mrs. Brewer — I cannot imagine why; I still think it just because the weather was so fine. Even the old fig tree at Woolmers bore to ripeness three out of seven fruit, of which the Admiral (always up early), had one, and Jessie (of necessity up even earlier), the other two. Mrs. Brewer in relating this added that she was fond of a fig herself, she always considered a fig quite a treat — which in an obscure way made me appreciate all the more her bringing me out a glass of sherry.

I sipped it, made it last, with I confess great enjoyment. I had never seen my garden look prettier with alyssum and snapdragons, nor my artichokes handsomer: it was the moment when their huge cobalt-blue thistle-heads were at the very peak of blueness — though to say "moment" is to do the plant an injustice. There is nothing flash-in-the pan about an artichoke; they would swagger in full glory in a week or two more.

5

The war was already ending. At last it ended. The bonfire lit on the heath, even if several ration books were tossed into it all too prematurely, nevertheless symbolized the triumph of light over darkness. I was particularly happy that Antoinette, whom I kept up to see the glow at least (the occasion so historic), wasn't frightened at all, only surprised and pleased. Of course she was used to quite spectacular sunsets — *see where Christ's blood streams in the firmament* — but never before had seen the heath where she rode her pony suddenly and inexplicably ablaze.

Not so long since, she'd have been frightened to the point of vomiting. Now she squirmed against me not in fear but in pleasure, and I could put her into bed, and go to bed myself, confident of a good night's sleep for us both.

As the war ended some of our pretty young wives (the lucky ones) welcomed back husbands safe and sound and moved away with them. Others were less lucky; but there was no such Spring-tide of mourning as I remembered in 1918. One husband who came back and stayed amongst us was Peter Amory, so disabled that to get his wife with child again from a wheelchair was another triumph of light over dark, over war and all that is against life, and I believe it was for this rather than for his medals the village regarded him as a hero.

6

Though Cecilia had connections, so evidently had many another impatient passenger, with civil airlines. The first Christmas of peace passed, then the New Year; it was spring again before she was able to set a date for seeking her only consolation — and even that not entirely firm. (*"If only my darling Rab were still alive!"* wrote Cecilia; by which I hoped she was realizing how much she owed him all round.) However I still felt it my duty to introduce into Antoinette's mind the notion that the war, of which she knew nothing, was over, and that a mother, of whom she had no more conception, was coming back to reclaim her.

I forced myself to make several attempts. —I say forced, because the notion of any change whatever (even from rice to tapioca, from cocoa to chocolate) so upset her; and indeed after a third attempt to introduce the prospect of a new mode of life altogether, she and I were so equally distressed, I cowardly gave up and leaned simply on the creed of blood calling to blood, as warranted by the Elizabethan dramatists.

Obviously Cecilia had connections of some sort; a good deal sooner than might have been expected, first by cable, then by telegram from London, then by word of mouth from Woolmers, I knew to expect Cecilia next afternoon.

As I have said, it was for mid-April cool but not cold, showery rather than rainy, and with that peculiarly autumnal tang in the air.

PART
TWO

6

We were quite a little reception committee to welcome her, as her car drew up outside the guest-house. I was there of course; the Vicar and his wife, who had been having tea with the Admiral, brought him out too, and several lesser lights happened to be passing by. —Any cable or telegram is naturally common, or rather uncommon news in our village, moreover Woolmers has the advantage (from the village point of view), of no drive; all the garden lying behind, the front door opens directly on the road, which makes it easy to keep a check on comings and goings. As interested spectators I noticed Mrs. Page representing the Mothers' Union, Miss Holmes the Women's Institute, and Mrs. Cook of the fish-and-chips representing trade.

It is often rash of a beauty to return, even after no more than a few years' absence, to her beauty's cradle. Beautiful women who move much about the world enjoy a constantly renewed meed of admiration, as heads turn in restaurants, on a promenade-deck, at spa or fashionable watering-place; but the time comes when heads no longer turn; whereas a beauty who stays at home may keep her reputation as such in the face of all contrary evidence. The first time Cecilia came back she was thirty-four: now she was almost forty, and such an interval often makes all the difference to a woman's looks. But however overdriven on behalf of Bundles for Britain, no such considerations need have troubled Cecilia: a beauty she left us, and a beauty she returned.

Her bare head, the hair a little darker, shone like a ripe chestnut; her complexion, a little paler, but slightly tanned — it transpired she had come via Bermuda — instead of cream-and-roses was an even lovelier cream-and-honey. As she stepped from the car and stood smiling before us in her big traveling-coat of violet-coloured wool, Mrs. Page, and Miss Holmes and Mrs. Cook, and the Gibsons and the Admiral, we all, there is no other word, feasted our eyes . . .

But Cecilia had eyes only for myself. Absolutely ignoring everyone else —

"Where's Tony?" she cried. "Where's my darling daughter?"

I explained I'd left Antoinette at home, thinking it better they should meet first by themselves; whereupon Cecilia instantly kissed me — her cheek smelled of gardenias — and drew me with her back into the car to drive the quarter of a mile farther. As I hadn't remembered Rab Guthrie so silent, no more did I now remember Cecilia so affectionate. However she was naturally happy and excited.

I suppose we were in the car no more than two or three minutes, but they were filled to overflowing with delightful impressions. She emanated an aura of vitality and luxury of which we had been as long deprived as we had of French scent, and which equally refreshed. —A fold of thick, soft, violet-coloured tweed lapping over my mackintosh, I could hardly refrain from fingering what I knew would be soft, springy texture of cloth undoubtedly woven in Scotland, but for years For Export Only. I have described the colour as violet, but there were all the tints of heather in it. It was more a rosy lavender and in the folds purple. I still do not find it absurd that I took such pleasure in a mere patch of cloth; and at the moment (drawing in the scent of gardenias as well), suddenly remembered a child in a marquee wide-eyed as at the kiss of a fairy princess; and felt it was perhaps like a fairy godmother Cecilia came back for Antoinette.

2

As we entered my sitting-room Mrs. Brewer, who I saw had been letting Antoinette help her shell peas, tactfully withdrew — or rather scuttled out. (I appreciated the effort it must have cost her; she scuttled sidelong, crabwise, her eyes — like a crab's almost on stalks.) Cecilia too showed great tact. She didn't swoop to press Antoinette to her bosom. She just stood tall and beautiful and smelling of gardenias as the child stared up at her, and said, "Hi, my darling!" It was I who made a fool of myself.

For the Elizabethan dramatists proved broken reeds. Naturally, in this case, the mother (Cecilia) knew the child; but the child Antoinette merely stared as at a complete stranger, also remained completely mute. —Thinking back, I realized that even had she pronounced her one complete sentence — *"Hello, in my rucksack I have pepper, vermin and a tureen"* — Cecilia might have been less impressed than disconcerted. At the moment I realized only that something had to be said, and so made a fool of myself.

"Look, Antoinette," said I, "here's your pretty mummy!"

Ready as I was to envisage Cecilia as a fairy godmother, even in my own ears the words rang false. Antoinette shifted her gaze to direct it upon me instead. I had never seen her give such an intelligent, searching look. Alas, it was also suspicious. Hitherto I'd never spoken a word to Antoinette she couldn't absolutely believe in; that she as often as not judged by tone rather than sense possibly helped her now to detect a falsity. She looked at me with — suspicion.

"And see what I've brought you!" exclaimed Cecilia.

It was a pretty thing indeed she produced from her big crocodile leather purse — another, littler purse, of pink silk embroidered with daisies, on a slim gilt chain. It was quite beautifully made, and obviously expensive, and to most little girls would no doubt have been a thing of joy. Antoinette regarded it without interest.

"And what will you give me, for this pretty thing?" enticed Cecilia.

Of course most children of eight are sophisticated in Forfeits, but it was still too difficult a game for Antoinette. She remained mute.

"A kiss?" suggested Cecilia, leaning with her hand outstretched in the very attitude I remembered so well. She had lost not a whit of her old grace! But Antoinette stood pat.

"She's shy," Cecilia told me. "Take it for free, honey!"

With which she put the purse into Antoinette's hands; who turned and took it out into the garden.

I thought Cecilia acted wonderfully well. She just laughed and shrugged her shoulders as amiably as possible. She didn't stay many minutes, even, longer; she was naturally tired, and when she said she meant to bribe the chambermaid at Woolmers to bring her dinner in bed, I didn't blame her.

"Though I'd intended to grab Tony straightaway!" she regretted. "It's what I've been promising myself! But perhaps not just to-night, would you say?"

Indeed I would, and we left it that she should instead return for Antoinette in the morning.

"When I'll tell you all my wonderful plans for her!" added Cecilia gaily.

As soon as she was gone I went out into the garden myself, but the child was nowhere to be seen. I looked in all her favourite haunts, such as up in the thicket and under the artichokes; no Antoinette. Of course she had her own ways of getting back into the house: where I found her at last was under her cot.

Her confidence in myself was restored soon enough. I persuaded her out into the garden again (where she was always most at ease), and let her squat or wander about, and repeated all our familiar rhymes, until a much later bedtime than usual. Thus I asked Antoinette's forgiveness, as I am quite sure she understood, though she remained grave and as it were judicious; she was sorry for me because I'd done something wrong; and if it seems absurd to attribute any such feelings to an innocent, I can only say that so it was, and that she forgave me because she was sorry for me. Properly (however belatedly) in bed after the Lord's Prayer she chimed in with vermin just as usual. Her confidence, as I say, was restored; which made it all the more difficult when I talked to Cecilia again next morning.

I was still hoping for a fairy godmother. If Antoinette had shown nothing but suspicion, who but myself was to blame, for having flinched before my duty of preparation? Might not Cinderella too, thought I, in the first moment of surprise, have taken the Good Fairy for a witch? But to turn rats into coach-horses is quite a different thing from turning them into psychiatrists.

7

Darling, what you've done for my infant I'll never, never be able to repay!" opened Cecilia warmly. "If it hadn't been *you* she was with I'd have just had to swim the Atlantic! But I always knew she couldn't be in better hands; and so did her father."

I said I was very happy to hear it. —We were by ourselves; I had let Antoinette go with Mrs. Brewer to see the Brewer rabbits, which though she'd seen scores of times already were perennially interesting to her. I felt it better that a conversation I foresaw as being important should be uninterrupted.

"And Mr. Hancock," added Cecilia — I thought not quite tactfully; it reminded me that despite Rab Guthrie's high opinion I had nonetheless been so to speak inspected . . .

"But now," went on Cecilia, looking more serious, "there must obviously be changes. *Physically* she looks wonderful — much, much *sturdier!* — and of course that's half the battle."

I could only imagine Cecilia had forgotten what her daughter looked like. Antoinette was always sturdy. However the implication that there was another half of the battle still to be won was entirely just, and I felt relieved that Cecilia seemed to show so much awareness. But when she added, almost in parenthesis, that her immediate plan was to take Antoinette straight back to New York by air, I was simply appalled.

Though I suppose I should have been prepared for this, I was not. As I told Mr. Hancock, and it was still true, Antoinette had never been even on a bus; such a transit as was now proposed, unless after long preparation, and then constant familiar reassurance *en route,* might well prove disastrous. That she would have her mother with her made no iota of difference, in view of the painful fact that her mother was still a total stranger.

So I saw that I'd have to speak plainly to Cecilia even sooner than I'd intended; only at that moment she jumped up and demanded to be shown where her babe had been sleeping. She'd tried so hard to picture it, she said, just as she'd tried so hard to picture every single minute of the day what Tony was doing at the same moment. —The time-lag between England and New York being I understand some five hours, I saw that indeed it must have been difficult, especially when Antoinette went to bed — in New York about midnight, plump in the middle of a Bundles for Britain Gala. I made no comment, however, and showed Cecilia upstairs. It was quite a pleasure to follow at her beautiful skirts of honey-coloured cashmere! But without her big traveling coat one saw that from being slender she had grown very thin, almost angular; so perhaps organizing galas was harder work than I'd imagined.

At the sight of Antoinette's cot extended by a piano-seat she appeared so appalled, I was only glad she hadn't been able to picture it. Personally I had grown too used to the contrivance even to notice it as such, but I dare say to Cecilia it looked like some makeshift in a slum.

"I could easily have got something bigger," I hastened to explain. "In fact, I once did; but Antoinette's very fond of her cot."

At that Cecilia smiled tolerantly.

"Such a babe, she was fond of Bridget too! — the Irish girl we had before Miss Swanson . . ."

"Miss Swanson who was so completely qualified?" asked I.

"Well, of course," said Cecilia. "She cost the earth, but she was worth it. —Who told you about her?"

"You did," said I. "That is, you mentioned her, the first time I saw Antoinette."

"What a memory!" exclaimed Cecilia. "Look, why not let's go down again, and I'll beg a coffee?"

She was very restless. It was a sort of interruption to our talk I hadn't bargained for. —Happening to glance out of the window, I moreover saw Antoinette and Mrs. Brewer prematurely returning. But I felt fairly sure Mrs. Brewer wouldn't bring the child indoors, and having really no option in any case took Cecilia back to the sitting-room.

It wasn't coffee I offered her, but sherry; actually from the bottle I'd opened for Doctor Alice. I have to make my sherry last! — but I was anxious to ingratiate myself with Cecilia in every possible way. Yet the nettle had to be grasped, and as soon as she was seated again, I grasped it.

"Of course you must realize," said I, "Antoinette isn't quite like other children?"

Cecilia paused to take a cigarette from her beautiful gold case; then snapped open her lighter.

"Of course she's terribly shy . . ."

I waited.

"If you mean almost mute — which isn't in the least the same thing as retarded — she was already having speech-therapy tuition from Miss Swanson. Didn't you hear me tell her father," added Cecilia rather righteously, "we should have left her behind? By now she'd be talking quite normally — or at least could have told me hello!"

I refrained from saying that Antoinette could additionally pronounce the words vermin, pepper, rucksack and tureen. Normal talk, that is, in Cecilia's sense, social talk, had small use for any one of them, except possibly pepper, in alliance with smoked salmon; tureen has disappeared along with large Victorian families, rucksack is overspecialized and vermin altogether out of court.

"I suppose we all make mistakes," said I.

"Not that I'm blaming you, not for a single moment," Cecilia reassured me generously. "It's just one of those things that sometimes seem to happen, and now we must just pick up the pieces."

Whereupon it developed that Antoinette, as soon as in New York, would not only be put into speech-therapy class again, but probably into analysis as well. —I looked over my shoulder into the garden; the artichoke-tops, though there was no wind, stirred a little, as though some small animal moved below. How to analyze mole or hedgehog, thought I, into any acceptably human behaviour? Yet I myself knew Antoinette not merely animal; all she needed to become fully human was simply time, and endless love, and endless patience, and no sudden uprooting — here I saw her as rather vegetable — from familiar ground . . .

It was now more than ever that I missed Doctor Alice. I felt she was the only person who could have made Cecilia see reason — or rather who might have bullied Cecilia into behaving reasonably. If my friend had been alive, to say, *"I, a qualified doctor, watched your daughter for two years, she is developing absolutely as fast as can be hoped, I warn you any sudden change of treatment or circumstances will be disastrous for her,"* then, I felt, Cecilia must have been influenced — especially if (in these imaginary conversations) I let Doctor Alice employ the curt, almost hectoring tone of voice she used to intimidate overweight pregnant mothers or anti-vivisectionists. But there was no one now with sufficient authority to intimidate Cecilia. The new (old) doctor had never set eyes on Antoinette.

So I suggested to Cecilia that after coming back amongst us after so long an absence, and obviously giving everyone so much pleasure at seeing her again, she should stay at least two or three weeks longer, and then have another word with the airline.

"As I shall in any case!" said Cecilia, suddenly abstracted and frowning. "Somewhere on the way across they lost me a spray of orchids from the freezer!"

With sudden hindsight I realized what of course had been the one thing lacking to complete Cecilia's image the day before. (Indeed I learned afterwards from Miss Holmes that Mrs. Cook, always an iconoclast, had actually exclaimed, "Wot, no orchids?" — but fortunately not loudly enough to be generally heard.)

"Besides," I went on, "though Antoinette obviously adores you already —" I was glad Antoinette wasn't present, to fix me with her searching eye again, but I was only doing my best for both of us— "for any child it's a very sudden change."

"You mean she should come and stay a little with me at Woolmers first?" responded Cecilia, quite reasonably.

"And have her cot in your room," said I. —It was by night Antoinette most needed the reassurance of familiarity, and her cot at least would be familiar, while she learned familiarity with a mother.

"But of course!" exclaimed Cecilia, seeming rather taken by the idea; and added that she'd just love to see

Tony say her prayers, in her nightdress. —It was obviously no moment to explain the futility of such expectations, Cecilia not yet being conditioned, as I was, to equate "vermin" with Amen; however by reminding her how exhausted she must still be after her flight, and how much in need of some further nights' unbroken rest, which with a small child in the same room was scarcely possible, I succeeded in postponing Antoinette's transference to Woolmers for a day or two more, even if it meant Cecilia's staying on a whole week.

"And even if I'm to be bored to death by that old sailor-man?" grimaced Cecilia — obviously referring to the Admiral, who'd apparently managed to bore her to death over a first breakfast at separate tables.

Then naturally she wanted to see Antoinette. I knew the child was back, and now in fact felt glad of it; I did not wish Cecilia to fancy any dog-in-the-mangerishness on my part. However as we went into the garden I remarked that the child was probably hiding — she often hid, and it sometimes took quite a while to find her. "Hide-and-seek? But that's perfect!" cried Cecilia. "Isn't it just what we must do, play together, while we make friends? —Count up to ten, Tony," she called lovingly, "then Mummy'll come and find you!"

That Antoinette couldn't count up to three was immaterial — though again I was dismayed by the scope of Cecilia's expectations — since she certainly knew how to hide. After several fruitless darts and dashes, however methodically Cecilia quartered the ground her quarry remained unflushed. The artichokes stirred again, but only at Cecilia's investigation, as so did the saplings on the terrace above, whence only a pigeon clattered out. With more patience, I dare say Cecilia might have discovered the secret route back to the house by way of the old coal cellar, but after about ten minutes she tired.

"Yoo-hoo, baby, I give you best!" called Cecilia. "Come out now and let Mummy hide!"

"I'm afraid she won't," I explained. "It's a very strict rule; you have to find her."

The idea of Antoinette playing any game whatever, especially according to rules, was naturally less surprising to Cecilia than to myself actually advancing it. Cecilia just laughed, and said she'd better go back to Woolmers to make sure of her room for a further week. The place being half empty, this was indeed superfluous, but I refrained from saying so.

As for Antoinette, she had been sick amongst the cinders. What extraordinarily touched me was that for the first time she had also attempted to clean up the mess herself — or rather to conceal it, by scraping more cinders on top. We were a grubby pair enough, we both needed a thorough wash, before we ate our lunch together in peace!

2

Mrs. Brewer was extremely apologetic about coming back so early, but had thought it better, on account of Bobby. The Parrishes were her next-door neighbours, and Bobby, who now spent most of his time at Ipswich, was home on holiday — or that was how his mother put it, as though it were from a boarding school, not a hospital, her luckless son from time to time reappeared. She was always crazing Doctor to let her have him home for good, commiserated Mrs. Brewer, and sometimes for weeks it answered well enough; but then he'd have another of his bad turns, perhaps two or three running, and have to be sent back . . .

"And it looked like he was starting one straight across the fence," said Mrs. Brewer, "so I brought Miss away."

I was only glad she had acted so sensibly. Antoinette was frightened enough already.

Yet to describe her as actually frightened by Cecilia would no doubt be an exaggeration. She disliked, even feared, any stranger — Janet Guthrie a rare exception; what was unfortunate was that the counterbalance of Cecilia's beauty weighed with her not a whit. What Antoinette found beautiful, or at least appreciated, was the grotesque — Kevin's squint, the hairy, warty old chin of Mrs. Bragg; she was like an art critic too besotted with Brueghel to see merit in the classicism of an Ingres, and thus Cecilia's universal *laissez-passer* of loveliness for once, with her own daughter, didn't advantage her.

8

But Cecilia was to stay a week at least, and I felt it a small victory; at the same time, having as it were promised her, offered as a bait, a social *succès fou,* was rather dismayed when I looked at my diary to see absolutely no Outdoor Fête or even Garden Party imminent for her to shine at. Before June is always a dull patch. All I had down, actually for a couple of days later, was the Women's Institute Auction in the Church Hall.

Which was really no more than a Jumble sale, only our village prefers the higher excitement — particularly our Old Age Pensioners, bidding in pence for the odd cup or plate; they do not want them for themselves, but to make presents of, which surely reflects great credit on human nature. I must possess at least a dozen cracked saucers so gifted to me, and very useful they are to put under a plant-pot, though not of course while watering. Sounder kitchenware and ironmongery fetch shillings, and garments with any wear left in them; whatever might fetch pounds goes to the proper Auction at the Estate Agent's. Thus I looked in the afternoon before simply from general nosiness, and was quite astonished to discover, tossed down on the Garments trestle, something really attractive.

It was an Oriental robe, or caftan, of thin lavender-and-purple striped silk which Colonel Packett (father of Honoria), had brought back with him from somewhere in the Empire, and which often figured in our Nativity Plays; he having recently died, I could only imagine it somehow cast up from the detritus of his effects. Honoria had made a very clean sweep. I didn't blame her, after years of polishing Benares brass trays when all she really enjoyed polishing was a stirrup. No one could blame Honoria, especially when I add that her father also kept Persian cats needing to be as regularly brushed as the trays to be polished. Though I cannot say I like Honoria, her punctual performance of all daughterly duties, in addition to running a riding stable, commanded my respect, and had I been a tycoon indeed I would have had no hesitation in hiring her.

To return to the caftan. —As I have said, nothing in our Jumble ever fetches more than shillings; but the garment was in itself so pretty, and could so easily do duty as a summer dressing-gown, I mentally determined to bid if necessary up to a guinea for it. In fact I was trying it on when I heard behind me the swish of Paul Amory's rubber-tired wheelchair.

He manages it with such wonderful skill one scarcely thinks of him as incapacitated at all, but rather as preferring a special, personal form of locomotion. —"Just as well!" observed Mrs. Brewer darkly: her implication, which indeed she did not hesitate to put into words, being that otherwise not a young woman in the place would be safe from him. This I am sure was unjust; Paul Amory is devoted to Betty; but at the same time he is very good-looking. Just before his hair needs cutting I am myself sometimes reminded of Byron. However what I even more admired about him was the courage and resolution with which he painted almost the worst water-colour landscapes I have ever seen.

"Ah!" said Paul, looking at me (and the caftan).

"It's agreeable, isn't it?" said I.

"Actually I'd an eye on it for Betty," said he. "She saw it this morning."

Of course everyone sees everything beforehand, but for a moment I was put out. Then I reflected how far more suitable the pretty, thin, voluminous garment to a pregnant young wife, especially with the summer coming; and said I'd just been trying it on in memory of Colonel Packett — there is nothing so foolish the young won't believe of the old — and had no intention to bid.

"Though you may have to go up to a pound," I warned (judging by my own impulse).

"I'll go up to thirty bob," declared Paul. "Betty's taken a fancy to it."

"Don't be too eager," I warned again, "and you may get it for ten!"

A moral dilemma ever attendant on our Jumble sales is whether to push the bidding up (so benefiting the Women's Institute) or let knock-down prices benefit one's neighbours. Mrs. Cook, for example, should never have got away with an electric kettle for seven-and-six. The proper Estate Agent sales are of course different — at one of which, I am happy to recall, in one of my tycoonish moods I outbid a London dealer for a Georgian silver sugar-bowl, and Georgian silver has gone up ever since. However I had no fear of Paul's being outbidden, if prepared to go above a pound; and didn't even bother to be there — see one Jumble, see all! — but stayed at home in the garden with Antoinette.

We were still at peace. The day intervening, Cecilia, after first her journey and then so much emotion, had to spend recuperating absolutely in bed; as I learned not only from Jessie (Mrs. Brewer's niece) but also from a note in Cecilia's own hand — *"Darlings both, forgive me, I'm just so tired!"* — pushed through my letter-box at mid-morning. Obviously it wasn't delivered by our postman, whose deliveries are strictly at eight-thirty and then at one. Mrs. Brewer said she'd seen the Admiral about.

Not that the Thursday had been entirely tranquil so far as I myself was concerned. We all knew Mrs. Bragg was failing, because for several Sundays running no milk had been stolen; but on Thursday just after breakfast our policeman arrived with a long face and asked if I'd mind going round till the undertaker sent a pro.; it didn't seem right she should be left, he explained, on account of the cats. "There's quite a comfortable chair," he added encouragingly, "and I've sprinkled a bit of disinfectant about . . ."

It was just as well. I am hardened to the disagreeable frowst of old people's sickrooms, where the first response to illness is often to close every window; but the stench in Mrs. Bragg's cottage was so to speak vintage. The whiff of her coat in the High Street but hinted at it. But at least it might be said that it wasn't old Mrs. Bragg herself, even in death, who stank, the smell of cat overriding all others.

Evidently the creatures hadn't been let out for some days, and so naturally had had to relieve themselves where they could. I propped the door wide open, but obviously too late in the day to interest them (cats having very regular motions); only one or two nosed out, and almost immediately slunk in again, as though half-starved into lethargy. I did the best I could for them by filling half-a-dozen bowls and pans with tap-water and setting them on the floor. The cats lapped, mewed for something more, and then when no better was forthcoming subsided into patches of thin parti-coloured fur, like old mats.

All this was before I looked at their owner. When I did, I saw easily why our policeman hadn't hesitated to summon the undertaker. Flat on the floor, flat on her back — nose sharp as a pen, mouth and eyes rigidly open — old Mrs. Bragg was obviously dead as a doornail. I saw no danger to her from the cats, from either affection or hunger; they gave the body a rather wide berth.

As our policeman had promised, there was a quite comfortable chair, an old-fashioned bentwood rocker which I actually recalled being knocked down at a Jumble for seven-and-six. It still had a sound cane back and seat; only I would have sat more comfortable in it had not every now and then, from the parti-coloured mats, a green or yellow eye opened . . .

Our policeman was as good as his word, however; only a couple of hours elapsed ere he came back with a smooth-voiced professional who — took over.

"And you'd better get the R.S.P.C.A.," said I.

What else to do with old Mrs. Bragg's cats, but have them put down? At least a dozen, that is; sparing a pair of Persians and their kit. At first I couldn't imagine how Mrs. Bragg came by them at all; then realized that Honoria had indeed made a clean sweep.

I am happy to say the R.S.P.C.A. found them good homes quite immediately; and that the kit in maturity, under the name of Felix Suffolk Braggart, took Second Best in Class at the Olympia, London, cat show.

3

The day of the Jumble itself I as I say stayed at home. I expected Cecilia at first in the morning, then at least by tea-time; but when at half-past five there was still no sign could only suppose her still recuperating, and put my garden shoes on.

East Anglia, especially near the coast, seems to have a climate of its own, and usually (or such is the general East Anglian belief), much better than anywhere else; warned in the papers *All Southeast England, cloudy,* we as often or not bask in unofficial sunshine. Even the calendar has less authority: though we were still only in May, the afternoon was so summer-hot, to step from the unshaded part of the terrace into the little copse was like going into a church — at least ten degrees cooler than outside. I greatly enjoyed the sensation, particularly as I was rather sweaty from separating catmint. (This should of course have been done earlier, but since I had Antoinette with me when was anything in my garden done by date?) The spicy scent clinging to my hands was peculiarly distinct above that rather muted, anonymous, twig-and-leaf smell which only in autumn develops a full bouquet; I was happy to look forward to that too, after the catmint gave up flowering . . .

Below me, as I glanced down, I could see Antoinette grubbing among the artichokes like some happy little animal. I must confess I should have been pleased if she in turn had looked up, and perhaps smiled, at me, but then what better proof of a little animal's complete trust than that it has learned to ignore one's presence?

Antoinette grubbed away contentedly. I loitered smelling the catmint on my hands, snapping off now and then a twig without a leaf-bud, observing with pleasure that a periwinkle (heeled in as untimely as I'd divided the catmint!) seemed to have decided to take root. Periwinkles are almost as favourite with me as artichokes — Tom Thumb and Prospero!

Looking down between the saplings a few minutes later, to see Antoinette still busy and absorbed, I also saw Cecilia.

She was wearing the caftan.

Its thin yet voluminous folds of lavender and purple silk softened all angularity; above them her beautiful head reared with an especial, flowerlike grace. She looked like a tall iris walking. I have never seen her look so lovely, nor so much at home in a garden.

4

Antoinette had seen her too. I watched almost holding my breath as the round fair head lifted, instinctively ducked, then raised again to stare longer at Cecilia swaying across the lawn like a tall iris . . .

The artichokes parted. Antoinette was coming out.

I held my breath as she, first, allowed herself to be seen, then step by cautious step advanced. Cecilia, the tall iris, had the wit not to speak, to stand quite still —

she too perhaps holding her breath? — only extended her hand, now empty of any bribe . . .

Unfortunately what Antoinette placed in it was a dead frog.

I do not blame Cecilia for screaming. Had I not once almost screamed myself, at the gift of a bullock's eye? Naturally Cecilia screamed. But she also slapped down Antoinette's hand, and as the little corpse dropped between them trampled it angrily, disgustedly underfoot; and then it was Antoinette screaming.

Of course I was beside them in a moment, and at the sight of me she stopped, but while I was still explaining to Cecilia that from Antoinette the gift of a dead frog was a mark of high esteem, as silently and suddenly as a mole or hedgehog the child disappeared, and I knew all too well where I should find her.

I must say Cecilia recovered herself very quickly. She made a great joke of it. "For heaven's sake, have I an infant biologist on my hands? Was she going to *dissect* it? Where on earth in New York am I going to find frogs for her?" cried Cecilia, in humorous mock dismay — so I myself tried to seem to take it as lightly. But I was in fact very much concerned that the first time Antoinette approached her mother of her own accord, and with a gift, should have ended in disaster. For disaster it was, since to Cecilia's offense in crushing the frog was added the offense of her screaming — the very reverse of any sound Antoinette could tolerate.

"At least this time I'm not going to play hide-and-seek with her!" declared Cecilia — now humorously revengeful. "Actually I'd come just to show you I'm on my feet again. You were right, darling — when aren't you? — I was tireder than I knew!"

Well, obviously she'd been on her feet long enough to get to the Jumble; and had come also, I thought, to display her new acquisition. It was only natural, when she looked so lovely in it; but however much I admired her in Colonel Packett's caftan (and however much I wanted to know how much she'd given for it), some perverseness made me refrain from comment. Nor did Cecilia draw attention to the garment — I suppose suddenly perceiving the same hole as I did in her explanation for not appearing earlier. We both behaved as though she wore nothing more out of the way than my own bagged skirt and darned cardigan — on my part, as I say, perversely: for even when I took her into the sitting-room for a glass of sherry I still had the impression of some lovely tall iris improbably strayed within doors . . .

As though now decided to make a social occasion of it, Cecilia was really wonderfully interesting and entertaining as she described all the Fancy Balls and Gala Concerts she'd organized in aid of Bundles for Britain; and touching, too, when she recalled Rab Guthrie's eighteen-hour working day that left him too exhausted to accompany her to any one of them. Often, it appeared, Cecilia herself returned quite exhausted in the small hours of the morning just as he was getting up and making himself coffee, so that for all the years of the war they'd scarcely seen each other. I felt very sorry for Rab Guthrie — particularly as no more had he seen his daughter on a pony.

"You must see Antoinette on a pony," said I.

"She rides? At least that's something," said Cecilia, "if she can ride in Central Park!"

I was especially pleased at this approval because I was already wondering how she and Antoinette had best re-encounter. On the heath Antoinette was always at her most normal, also there would be Honoria and the young Cockers throwing out so to speak a protective screen. Even when I told Cecilia the next lesson wasn't till Tuesday, quite towards the end of the week she'd promised us, she seemed undisturbed, as though prepared to stay even longer. I wondered whether she too, under her lightness, had recognized a setback and the need for patience. She didn't recur, for instance, to her plan to transfer Antoinette immediately to Woolmers. In short, I felt much encouraged; and we parted on such good terms, I was hardly surprised when for the second time Cecilia kissed me.

"You will help?" breathed Cecilia. "Only you can, you know. You will help — both of us?"

5

Antoinette was where I expected; under her cot. This time I spoke to her rather firmly — not loudly, of course, but more firmly than usual. "Come out, Antoinette," I told her. "I'm sorry, and Mummy's sorry; but it was just an accident, and you mustn't be such a baby any more . . ."

From the darkness under the cot Antoinette's small bright eyes regarded me unwinkingly.

"Come out at once, Antoinette!" said I.

She came. She crept out very slowly, but she came. —It was from this time that I noticed a sort of docility quite new in her. She seemed to feel she was being punished for something, but didn't know what; so that her only resort was strict obedience. I confess it cut me to the heart that as Antoinette's first human expression had been one of suspicion, her second was of resignation. But time and events had overtaken us.

6

What Cecilia paid for the caftan turned out to be five guineas — thanks to which the takings of the Jumble reached the unprecedented figure of nine pounds fifteen and ten. I was still sorry for Paul Amory's disappointment, and meeting him next morning in the High Street took the opportunity to say so. —One meets everyone in the High Street, and Paul in his wheelchair is particularly, even if one wished to avoid him, as I did not, unavoidable.

"I'm sorry about the caftan," said I.

"So is Betty," said he, "but I went up to four quid. Then Mrs. Guthrie jumped."

He nonetheless sounded, and looked, less chagrined than one would have expected. In fact he appeared rather stimulated.

"D'you know what?" added Paul. "She's going to

let me have a shot at her portrait. We had a bit of a chat together afterwards — she made quite a joke of our being rivals! — and she's such a stunner, I couldn't help asking."

"I don't blame you," said I.

"And she's promised to let me try," rejoiced Paul, "even if it takes a month!"

9

Even a week's respite had heartened me; a month includes four. I only wondered how Betty would view a prospect to me personally so welcome, but she declared herself quite delighted at her husband's branching out; for to do justice to a portrait of Cecilia, Paul Amory launched from water-colours into oils. (As he naïvely explained to me, he knew how, he'd done oils — this rather in the tone of a boy saying he'd done algebra.) Of course oil is a more expensive medium, but though I suspect Betty had to keep house more narrowly she never complained, even when the marble slab she used for pastry making was commandeered as a substitute palette. For water-colours, Paul in his wheelchair had managed very handily with his sketch-block propped on a sort of reading desk hinged to its footrest, and a jam-jar of water slung from one arm and his paintbox on his knees; but oils are more demanding. To support a canvas there had to be an easel set up; the marble slab required a table of its own. All this naturally made a great clutter in the sitting-room of a cottage as small as the Amorys', as Cecilia was quick to realize; after a very few sittings all artistic paraphernalia was shifted to an empty garage at Woolmers. With petrol rationing still in force few visitors brought cars, and she may even have paid for its use. Paul openly rejoiced at having something so like a proper studio of his own, and out of Betty's way; nothing however could have been more public, since the doors were necessarily kept wide open, for light. Fortunately they faced east, and in the mornings, with side windows as well, the garage was all that a studio should be.

So Cecilia quite settled in, and spoke no more of any immediate departure. Indeed she began to talk quite as though she expected to spend the whole summer amongst us; she hadn't realized, she declared, how much she'd enjoy being home again! The words gave me such hope as I hardly dared examine — what if Cecilia decided to stay in England for good? — and in East Anglia, within reach? For Antoinette it would be like a miracle; but miracles have happened. Naturally — as I say, I hardly dared examine the thought — I made no such premature suggestion to Cecilia; but still took the opportunity to remark that now there was more time, perhaps Antoinette might as well stay where she was used to being for a little longer.

"You asked me to help," I reminded.

Cecilia looked serious but not uncooperative.

"You think it would? You don't think Tony might *resent* my not wanting to have her straightaway?"

I said no.

"You don't think it might give her a trauma?" persisted Cecilia.

Again, though the psychoanalytic term was then unfamiliar to me, I said no. I was in fact simply saying no to any doubts of Cecilia's whatever; and indeed without much further difficulty persuaded her to leave Antoinette a little longer where she was, and where Cecilia could so easily come and see her every day.

As things turned out it was in my garden, not on the heath, that mother and child re-encountered; Antoinette's Tuesday riding lesson never took place because Honoria went off to London. She had some business with her father's solicitor, also she took his medals to sell at Spinks, and one of them (dating from the Boxer Rising) fetched such an unexpectedly high price, Honoria stayed on in town going to theatres and looking up old chums for a full month. Of course she left a locum, a superannuated carter who saw to the ponies in the way of feeding and grooming, but neither Mrs. Cocker nor I had sufficient confidence in the old gaffer to let him lead out a juvenile string. Antoinette and the young Cockers missed eight riding classes running.

I didn't blame Honoria, but I was put out. Apart from the importance of that first, missed occasion, Antoinette enjoyed her riding. Now we just had to wait until Honoria returned from the fleshpots.

However, my garden was at least home ground, and Antoinette didn't a second time actually hide from her mother. It was part of her new docility that when I said (firmly), "Look, Antoinette, here's your pretty mummy come to see us, you're to stay and say hello to her and not run away," — Antoinette stayed.

She stayed perplexed and resigned; but she stayed. Once, later, of her own accord she showed me her hands, empty of any treasure . . .

Cecilia's visits were paid each morning either before or after her sitting, so she could never stay long; but still as everyone knew she saw her daughter every day. The very briefness of these descents was in fact an advantage, as not overstraining Antoinette's passive obedience; to Cecilia's loving "Hi there, honey!" or "Hi there, my darling!" Antoinette never failed to return the hello she'd learned riding with the Cockers — this pleased Cecilia very much — and then stood silently listening to Cecilia's chatter, or obediently followed her round the garden, for never longer than half-an-hour. Cecilia chattered so much Antoinette's silence was hardly apparent; indeed I remember Mrs. Gibson once telling me how pleased she'd been, passing by on the other side of the hedge, to hear the pair getting on so famously.

I understand there was great admiration for Cecilia's tact and sympathy at this point, she so fully recognizing how kind and useful I'd been to Antoinette that she was prepared not to reclaim her darling daughter quite there and then. Everyone knew (added Mrs. Gibson), how attached I was to the child, which in fact they did not.

2

There was no doubt that Paul Amory's new paints and brushes, and his new easel and new studio, did him a lot of good. He had always been cheerful, in a resolute sort of way, but now there was such a light of enthusiasm in his eye that even immediately after a haircut he looked more than ever Byronic, and returned home to lunch — (he always, however long a sitting overran its time, went home to lunch, which Betty kept hot for him) — in wonderfully high spirits.

But this was only one example of the pleasure that Cecilia, by her mere presence, brought amongst us. The war had been won by glum fortitude; everyone was tired. In London, one heard, as soon as the bombings stopped all anyone wanted to do was go to bed early. We in East Anglia, for the most part able to sleep our fill, and with nothing to keep us up, had on the contrary so overslept as to become dull as our neighbouring Norfolk's dumplings; it was astonishing how soon Cecilia revived a little spirit of gaiety and sociability amongst us. Besides beauty, she brought vitality; it emanated from her like the scent of gardenias. (French, of which we had been so long deprived.) Her very clothes — nothing patched or makeshift — after years of austerity were a treat for sore eyes; have I not described what almost sensual pleasure I myself derived from a fold of violet-coloured tweed? Thus Cecilia moved amongst us a heartening reminder of all the luxuries of peace, and by her mere presence promoted quite a round of unaccustomed gaieties.

The Cockers gave little dinner-parties for her, based on rare lobsters or else soles. For men, besides Sir David, they could always invite the U.S. Air Force Colonel, who with typical American generosity often contributed (and left behind unemptied) a bottle of Scotch. (Only delicacy, I feel sure, prevented his providing solids; he'd taken the pains to find out that seafood was off-ration.) Naturally Cecilia had a great success with him; besides her beauty and charm, wasn't she by marriage a compatriot? Soon the American Colonel was driving her to The Mariners' Arms and the Crown and Sceptre just as Rab Guthrie had done. But he was a married man with a wallet full of photographs of his wife and family.

As the weather warmed the American swimming pool too became very pleasant to Cecilia. I have said that on Saturday afternoons it attracted all the small fry of the village; Cecilia had carte blanche to patronize it whenever she liked, and take anyone she liked with her. The Colonel absolutely insisted that she take an escort — (how charmingly precise American grammatical usage!) — warning her of nine feet at the deep end. Actually Cecilia's delight, especially with anyone watching, was to run down over the shingle-ridge into the estuary itself where she could swim looking more like a mermaid. She often urged me to bring

Antoinette, to learn to swim too — of course in the pool; but I always managed some excuse. I could give even myself no real reason; what matter that I myself couldn't swim, the child's mother swimming so well? (Though I always felt more showily than strongly; Cecilia's butterfly-stroke was a marvel to behold, but only for about twenty yards.) Moreover now that her riding lessons were suspended, didn't she need some other wholesome exercise, and in company with her peers? My instinct was still to keep Antoinette — the little land-animal, the little mole or hedgehog — away from water; and in any case Cecilia never patronized the pool on Saturdays.

During the week, other escort lacking, she took the Admiral on guard duty. He once confided to me that the sight of Cecilia breasting the estuary was the most poetical damn' thing he'd ever seen in his life. There is no doubt that she spread a very great deal of pleasure — and not amongst new admirers only; old ones too came in for their share, as witness Major Cochran and Henry Pyke, each with his own senti-mental tale to relate.

In one way these were curiously alike, for both centered not so much on Cecilia herself as on the memories she'd aroused. Henry Pyke Cecilia reminded of his mother. I was surprised. According to Mrs. Brewer, with a memory even longer than my own, poor young Mrs. Pyke had been a bit of a weakling: pretty as a picture, but with no more guts to her than a drawn hen. Thus my impression was of some helpless pre-

Raphaelite beauty — even though it wasn't till she'd died that the thrashings (that left our own Henry Pyke a tongue-tied lameter), really began. "So long as she lived, 'twas never the strap," admitted Mrs. Brewer — but for once I thought slightly blaming someone, if only for having died young.

"But why should he have been thrashed at all?" I remember asking. "Was he so wild?"

"No; but puny," said Mrs. Brewer.

The East Anglian is a hard coast. Under all surface tolerance runs a hard streak; almost our only folk-hero is Peter Grimes. Old Henry Pyke, East-Anglian born and bred, had survived to grow in turn as hard-handed as his father; but he hadn't been so thrashed until his gentle mother died, and upon reflection I saw Cecilia's beauty and grace simply fitting into the shape of a boyish icon . . .

Major Cochran, ex-R.A., D.S.O. and bar, was reminded of a first love in India, for his Colonel's daughter, he no more than a subaltern with nothing but his pay. It seemed Cecilia had just the same stunning carriage and air of being more than common clay. "I dare say it wasn't more than once or twice I even partnered her in the mixed doubles," confided Major Cochran, "but I think she knew how I felt about her. Then of course she married a chap in the Hussars . . ."

That Cecilia should at one and the same time have reminded Henry Pyke of his mother and the Major of his Colonel's daughter — types of womanhood apparently as opposed as possible — didn't surprise me. In my considered opinion most men are fools sentimentally. But I wondered that neither had attempted to marry her before she married Rab Guthrie. They were neither of them in the category of Bank Managers or County Surveyors or even the average gentleman-farmer: Henry Pyke after all his thrashings inherited more than substantially, and Major Cochran too came into money — so much that had an uncle died sooner he might have challenged the chap in the Hussars. Yet neither, to my knowledge, ever proposed to Cecilia. Possibly they'd felt themselves, even so many years ago, too old for her, I meditated; and Mrs. Brewer (the topic somehow arising as we made my bed) agreed, though in cruder terms. Old fools they might have been the pair of them, said Mrs. Brewer, but still with a bottom of sense left . . .

I dare say it was the same bottom of sense that preserved them from singeing their wings and hearts afresh. Neither, for instance, went much out of his way to meet Cecilia in the High Street. But if an encounter chanced, what pleasure illumined each leathery old phiz! Also Major Cochran went into Ipswich to have his dentures seen to, and Henry Pyke let Scouts camp in his orchard.

Neither in any case was capable of doing guard duty at the swimming pool, nor could Paul Amory in his wheelchair attempt the mile and a half of shingly approach; but another returning young husband, Group Captain Pennon, was soon on the roster, and both he and his wife Janice swam very well.

How flattering it is, to the old, to be liked by the young! Even though they may have no more experience of life than a chicken in its shell, their liking still, however irrationally, flatters. When Janice told me I reminded her of Jane Austen I knew the comparison with that elegant moralist simply absurd, and put it down to a hangover from having read Eng. lit. at some provincial university; but was still flattered!

Her husband too had a slight provincial accent. (East Anglians never consider their own accent provincial. It is simply East Anglian.) I felt a great admiration for Peter Pennon, returned from what heroic battling in the skies to settle contentedly amongst us as a vet. In fact I once expressed it to him. He grinned and turned the conversation, but I think wasn't displeased, and no more was Janice. In short the Pennons and I liked each other, and became friends.

3

Cecilia in fact spread more pleasure than she was aware of. I have described the pretty purse brought for her daughter all the way across the Atlantic; after Antoinette took it out into the garden, it disappeared. For days I hunted about, at first expecting to find it simply dropped somewhere. (That I then looked under the artichokes was probably foolish; the cache scraped there by Antoinette was for treasures — an empty black-and-amber snail shell, an unusually striated pebble.) I also kept an eye open about the house, still without result. Then some time later Mrs. Brewer reported that squinty Kevin had got a girl to go to the movies with him at last, he having given her a lovely embroidered bag on a gilt chain. It was certainly a prettier present than a bullock's eye!

I was very grateful to Cecilia for her discretion in not asking what became of the toy, since I could not believe she had entirely forgotten it. I thought she behaved extremely well; and more than ever looked forward, as a sort of return favour, to showing her Antoinette on pony-back. Afterwards, of course, I could only wish Honoria had stayed in London.

10

But back Honoria came, greatly smartened up with lipstick and a new tweed coat, full of the shows she'd seen and the old chums she'd met, yet still quite glad, she whinnied, to be back with us old stick-in-the-muds. She found the ponies in good condition, though the saddlery was a bit of a mess, and on the first Tuesday after her return off we all set again, she and I and Antoinette and the three Cocker children, and now Cecilia of course accompanying.

To begin with all went quite splendidly. Just as I'd hoped, she was obviously pleased to see how well her daughter sat, and how readily and intelligently she exchanged a "hello" with the young Cockers, who on their part showed Antoinette a new regard for having such a beautiful mother. Everyone we passed looked at Cecilia admiringly. One or two faces even appeared at windows. As a rule our passage to the heath was simply a matter of getting there as fast as possible without trotting, and certainly attracted no attention, but with Cecilia accompanying it became quite a little procession!

The heath once gained, off the whole juvenile string first trotted, then cantered — Antoinette cantering with the best, and for once perfectly indistinguishable from any other child of her years. Naturally Cecilia couldn't realize what a triumph this represented, but there was no doubt of her pleasure; for once she looked even proud of her daughter. —Then suddenly Pepper stumbled, and Antoinette lost her stirrup and went headfirst into a gorse bush.

It was the most minor of misadventures. Honoria recovered both child and pony in a matter of moments, and Antoinette was no more than scratched. But beside me I felt Cecilia stiffen. I suppose it was rather incoherently that I tried to explain that Antoinette wasn't so much learning to ride — which indeed she was doing very well — as to mix with her peers; in any case Cecilia (all her maternal instincts aroused) listened to me no more than to Honoria. In vain did Honoria protest that Antoinette must at once remount, or the kid would lose her nerve; her loud neighings merely irritated Cecilia — as they had often done myself, but this time I felt them warranted: Antoinette flinched not in the least from Pepper (now closehauled on the leading-rein), only from her mother's hand on her wrist . . .

"What I absolutely refuse," declared Cecilia furiously, "is to have my child's nose broken!"

"But if she waits till next time out —" began Honoria.

"There won't be a next time!" snapped Cecilia.

She wouldn't even allow Antoinette to ride back. We returned from the heath — that is, Cecilia and I and Antoinette returned — on foot. I was chagrined to see the young Cockers looking no longer regardful but derisive. From a canter they broke spontaneously into a show-off gallop, and Honoria for once allowed it.

Cooling down, Cecilia assured me she didn't blame me in the least for my well-meaning if ill-judged experiment. She just felt more and more strongly that the sooner she herself took charge of her daughter the better, and that Antoinette's joining her at Woolmers, already too long delayed, must take place immediately.

"In fact, tomorrow," ordered Cecilia.

Who was I to argue? Though Antoinette, as I have said, was barely scratched, and though the trudge home, in jodhpurs and heavy shoes, was obviously more depleting than even another tumble could have been, who was I to argue? — especially when Cecilia, warming up again, presented it as sheer luck that every bone in the child's body hadn't been broken, let alone the bridge of her nose. So I simply said I would have Antoinette's cot sent round in the morning, and then bring Antoinette.

How much of these exchanges Antoinette herself comprehended I wasn't sure. Cecilia was speaking in a rather loud voice; from the child's expression, or lack of it, Antoinette might have been experimentally closing her ears. That she remained mute meant nothing — wasn't she normally mute? However Cecilia, insofar as she considered her daughter an interested party in the matter, undoubtedly took silence for consent.

"Good-bye for now, honey!" called Cecilia, quite gaily, as we parted at my gate. "Tomorrow you're coming to Mummy for always!"

All the rest of the morning, as a treat, Antoinette and I played tiddlywinks with rabbit-droppings.

She played — docilely; because I suggested it. When as an extra treat I let her have supper as well as lunch in the garden, with no more than the same docility did she follow me as I carried our trays out. However much, or little, she'd comprehended, of my conversation with Cecilia, I felt her still taking refuge in strict obedience.

How often, under the stress of emotion, the tongue turns to banality! (Or else to unnatural elaboration; I remember once, as a girl, driving with my father and his curate, being halted by a desperate, bloodied figure standing by the wreck of an overturned car in which someone screamed like a tailored hare. "Is either of you gentlemen," he asked, "a member of the medical profession?") In my own case, the words were banal.

"Tomorrow you're going to stay with your pretty mummy!" I told Antoinette.

It wasn't searchingly she looked at me, this time, but — resignedly.

"In a lovely great big house just down the hill!" I babbled on. "In your own bed, with your own mummy! Won't that be nice?"

Of course she didn't answer. I didn't expect her to. But I was sure she had indeed comprehended, and that I need babble on no more.

So I fell silent as she. Even to repeat her favourite poetry to her, at that juncture, would have been no more than babbling. Mrs. Brewer gone, the silence of the house became absolute. As a rule Antoinette and I could be silent together so companionably, words or no words made scant difference; now, such was the constraint between us, I found myself trying to think of something to say.

Resignation belongs properly to the middle years. I myself was I suppose forty before I resigned myself to my humdrum lot. In one's thirties, one still hopes. But to be resigned to one's lot as a child is terrible. I wondered whether Mr. Pyke had been resigned to his lot, under his father's thrashings? It seemed only too possible; also to think of so unbearable, I determined to make a last bid on Cecilia's patience, to persuade her to leave Antoinette with me even a few weeks longer; and why I failed is for a reason I still dislike to recall.

2

Next morning I went down to Woolmers early, and alone, on the pretext of seeing whether there was space in Cecilia's room not only for Antoinette's cot but also for her steamer trunk. —Of course there was space, Cecilia having the biggest single room in the guest-house; but what was my surprise to see a second bed installed already. Not a cot, but a bed. An adult's bed, very prettily counterpaned in pink chintz, with an extra pink cushion at the head, altogether most agreeable, but not a cot.

If I had been thinking more clearly, I must have realized that to Cecilia (unused to any sort of make-shift), no piano-stool extension would be acceptable for a moment; naturally she'd take her own measures, and in a guest-house easily enough. But it was extremely inconsiderate that she hadn't warned me the day before. I might well have had at least the stool with me there and then.

"*Now* isn't Tony going to be comfortable?" smiled Cecilia, looking if anything pleased at my surprise.

It was a bad beginning. If on the one hand my resolve was strengthened by the thought of Antoinette bereft even of her familiar sleeping-place, on the other Cecilia's complacency so irritated me I was afraid of losing my temper too soon. I was fully prepared to lose my temper if necessary — if necessary to hector Cecilia just as I'd imagined Doctor Alice hectoring her, calling upon, instead of medical authority, the tycoon or fish-wife side of my nature. But first I meant to advance every viable argument — such as Antoinette's obvious contentment, and improvement, where she was, her dislike, even fear, of every sort of change, and the ill consequences that might follow from any prematurely brought about. Sitting on the foot of the pink bed I began quietly and reasonably to advance them — until Cecilia, at my first pause, observed that it was of course twenty pounds a month.

To do her justice, I believe she almost immediately wished the words unuttered — so swiftly did she swoop towards me, and take both my hands between her own, and protest how well she knew no money could ever, ever repay all I'd done for her darling lamb. But spoken the words had been; and I, in an uncontrollable movement of false pride (since it was to be paid for by Antoinette) went away.

3

Our separation now inevitable, the last thing I desired, what I desired above all to avoid, was any emotional scene. I confess I was still hurt by the extreme composure — so complete as to seem to make foolish all my apprehensions — with which Antoinette, when the moment came, accepted her transference. Her small, round, Dutch face was expressionless absolutely; merely composed. She walked beside me down the hill to Woolmers for once without holding my hand; and when I left her there with Cecilia, it was only I who looked back.

All her toys — that is all her proper, New York-originating toys — of course went with her, though some had to be quite searched for, but no dead frog, or turd, did Antoinette make any attempt to smuggle.

It seemed as though she could shrug off a whole way of life (myself included) as easily as ever; as easily as five years earlier she'd shrugged off the life with her parents on the other side of the Atlantic . . .

"Let me learn from babes and sucklings!" thought I; and spent the rest of the day dismantling Antoinette's cot ready to be returned to the Women's Institute, also collecting innumerable paper napkins from behind cushions in the sitting-room. This was not to remove all traces of my child, but simply a rational tidying up. To cut down the artichokes would have been pure sentimentality, and I am happy to say I refrained; indeed at the end of my labours I went out and stood for quite some time amongst them.

It was a beautiful evening. We were now towards the end of May, and in early summer, in East Anglia, if the weather is fine — that is, if we are neither flooded nor frozen — even to draw breath is an uncovenanted blessing. To say that we breathe the best air in England is an understatement: we breathe the best air in the world. It comes straight to us from the North Pole, just sufficiently tempered by a ricochet off Holland: a few deep breaths on rising and one is set up for the day. In fact one is continually being set up, as well as toughened.

All the plants in my garden are tough. In years I had lost nothing but fritillaries — and they strangers to our parts with which I was foolish to experiment; big white daisies and pinks, clematis and mock orange, throve year after year in sturdy independence of temperature or mismanagement. My artichokes whether cut down or left to rot each year towered higher; the chunks of catmint I'd separated were already rooting. In fact the character of my garden was so to speak durability; and who more blessed than I enjoying both a durable garden and incalculable weather?

It had been an error to attempt the fritillaries. Not all plants transplant as easily as catmint; only the hardier, less uncommon sorts that have nothing special about them and need no especial care.

Incalculable indeed is our weather; even as I noted the temperature just about right (here I speak as my father's daughter!) to *chambrer* a bottle of claret, a sudden cooler breath in the air suggested hock, and overhead a rising cloudbank rain. Nothing could be more welcome; we needed rain; and I felt myself more than ever blessed in the accident of my habitation. Re-entering the house — now properly tidy again, no danger of treading on a dead frog! — I indeed quite brimmed with satisfaction at my lot in general; yet still welcomed the distraction of dining at the Cockers'.

As I have said, I dined with the Cockers on about two occasions in the year, and that evening rather fortunately happened to be one of them. As usual they had offered to send their car for me; as usual I had refused, preferring the independence of Alfred's taxi; and though for once it was late, having been to Ipswich to meet a train, I scarcely noticed. For once I had time. For once I had time to take a bath and make myself presentable. —Or even more than presentable, so I flattered myself, now having time also to brush my hair (which I can still sit on) into a proper pompadour, and to choose between the jet and amber necklaces inherited from my mother. I in fact wore the amber, as more lightening to my only dinner gown (grey). Actually it was so long since I'd made any sort of *toilette,* Alfred regarded me quite in surprise, but also with approval. "Nice change," he remarked; and promised to be there waiting for me even if later than usual. I thanked him, but said strictly ten o'clock.

It seemed strange to go out and leave the house dark — no light in any window to show even Mrs. Brewer in charge. It was strange to lock the door behind me because the house was empty. But it also, as Alfred said, made a nice change.

I thought I might even learn Greek.

11

Owing to Alfred's lateness, when I entered the Cocker drawing-room all the other guests were already assembled: the Admiral, our local M.P. and his wife, the American Colonel, and — Cecilia.

I was so astonished, I barely apologized to my hostess, and let myself be introduced to Mrs. M.P., before I asked, where was Antoinette?

"In bed, of course!" said Cecilia lightly.

"At Woolmers?" I asked foolishly.

"Where else?" returned Cecilia — very naturally with some slight impatience. "Not to worry, darling; I've bribed a chambermaid — Jane, or is it Jessie? — to keep an eye on her . . ."

Of course I knew it was Jessie, and a very nice, kind girl she was. But Antoinette didn't know her. To Antoinette, perhaps waking in the night, the face of Jessie would be as strange as all the rest of her new, strange surroundings; and if Antoinette woke in the night what she needed above all was the reassurance of the familiar.

"One must begin as one means to go on," added Cecilia. "I don't suppose even *you* sat up all night by her pillow?"

In point of fact, during the first weeks Antoinette was with me, it was exactly what I had done. For a moment my impulse was to turn round and walk straight out again — walk if necessary, if my taxi had gone, the whole two miles back to Woolmers. Then I remembered Antoinette's utter composure at our parting, and asked myself whether Cecilia's method might not after all be the right one, and stayed.

It was really a most agreeable dinner-party. The food (as always at the Cockers), was both excellent and off-ration, so that one felt no guilt at enjoying it: green pea soup made from fresh green peas followed by salmon-trout with new potatoes and an equally fresh green salad, followed by mushrooms on toast. I will not say the conversation actually sparkled, but it was interesting: I had never known Sir David so entertaining; he and the American Colonel between them covered almost three generations of warfare by land and sea and air, and each had many anecdotes to relate — the Admiral of a last brush with pirates off Hong Kong, the Colonel of raids as deep into enemy territory as Berlin itself. I found these exchanges quite fascinating — as of an ironclad signaling to an aircraft carrier — but enjoyed even more the discovery that the M.P.'s wife, like myself, knew Henry James almost by heart. We had barely time to get down to *Portrait of a Lady* — (was or wasn't the little daughter such an innocent as she seemed?) — before the mushrooms on toast.

Cecilia was of course enjoying the party too. However interested in each other's conversation, both warriors were intensely aware of her. How should they not be, she lending such grace and animation to the feast? In fact it was actually during this evening that I first perceived the Admiral to have his eye — there was no other phrase for it — on Cecilia.

Of course they met daily and all day at Woolmers; but he could never before have seen her in a low-cut black velvet dinner dress with diamonds in her ears. (Black for mourning, diamonds equally a tribute to so good a husband.) Thus Sir David's glances of extra admiration, so to speak, were easily explicable. What suddenly struck myself was that they had also a quality of speculation. I do not in the least mean to imply that his motives were mercenary — I am sure they were not; I guessed her money more of a stumbling block — but it forcibly occurred to me that during the watches of some night — about two bells — Sir David (still seaworthy) had hauled up to the notion of making Cecilia his wife.

Cecilia for her part was far more flirtatious with the American Colonel, which in the Admiral's place I would have taken for a good sign, that is if he knew anything about women, which I doubted. And indeed, upon consideration (over the salad), why should not

Cecilia, I thought be simply flirting with a more attractive male? Rich, beautiful and leader of New York Society as she was already, what had the Admiral to offer — except to make her My Lady? Then I remembered the incident of the bouquet stolen from Lady A.; and allowed Sir David a better chance . . .

Altogether it was a most interesting and enjoyable evening. I still left at ten, before the party settled down to cards. The Cockers made no attempt to detain me. They believed I couldn't afford their stakes; which was true, but by no means the whole truth. I have always felt I possessed remarkable card sense, hitherto so unextended in the mild rubbers played with my parents and a curate, I contrived to be dummy whenever possible. I should have played at Crockford's, at a guinea a point, or taken the bank at chemin-de-fer at Monte Carlo — and let the Greek syndicate beware! (*"Mon dieu! Voici l'Anglaise!"* I heard them mutter!) The latter scene was so vivid before my mental eye, however high (in their own view) the Cockers and their friends might play, I personally saw them as staking no more than rabbit-droppings; and really couldn't have been bothered.

2

Outside it was raining already (as I had suspected it would be), and Alfred putting me down at the gate congratulated me on having hired him, also advised a nice hot cup of cocoa before turning in. Actually the kind Crockers had given me a brandy, to follow up which with cocoa would have seemed to my dear father a blasphemy — if not a glass of Malvern water, then just plain tap. However I appreciated Alfred's kind thought to the extent of tipping him a shilling, which I do not always do. I was in a pleasantly relaxed mood altogether. Then he drove off through the rain, and I got out my key and walked cheerfully up to my front door.

Where crouched against the step like a little animal — her hands like little paws clutching at the sill — huddled Antoinette.

She must have tried to get in, as well, by the cellar, for her nightgown and bedroom slippers were grimed with coal dust. She had no coat or even dressing-gown; when I gathered her up I felt her damp to the skin. She didn't speak to me, just clung. I doubt whether she was quite conscious.

I took her in, and when I had washed and warmed her, and put her into one of my own flannel night-dresses, followed Alfred's advice and brewed a nice hot cup of cocoa; and then I took her back.

It was the hardest thing I ever did in my life. But consider: how might not such a disastrous beginning have affected the entire future? Cecilia was a person so used to success in all her schemes, the blatant, public failure of one so particularly near her heart I believed would arouse not only disappointment and chagrin, but resentment, and even anger. Though I might leave word at Woolmers, so that Cecilia, returning to an empty room, at least shouldn't be thrown into alarm, the fact remained that Antoinette had run away. Somehow Antoinette had got out, and through the dark and the rain run away from her mother back to myself. Undoubtedly Cecilia would be angry — and even after her anger cooled, perhaps find the rebuff as hard to forget as to forgive; so I took Antoinette back.

I felt fairly sure no one had seen her. Our village keeps early hours, and even uphill, even for a child, from the guest-house to mine is no more than ten or fifteen minutes. Obviously no one had seen her, or she would have been stopped. It occurred to me that if I could get her back and into bed before Cecilia returned, Cecilia might be kept in ignorance altogether. So I took Antoinette back.

Again, as earlier in the day, she made no struggle; and fortunately I am stronger than I look: I had to carry her. —It was still before eleven, and Woolmers' front door still unbolted, but I knew my way about well enough to use the back, and the back stairs as well, and the only person I met was Jessie. She had the grace to look thoroughly ashamed of herself, though protesting she'd left the child no more than two shakes and sleeping like a lamb. "And don't all innocents wander a bit by night? 'Tis their nature, and never come to harm," Jessie defended herself. I could have boxed her ears; but at least I knew she wouldn't talk.

I put Antoinette into one of her own nightgowns, and back into her strange bed — not so strange as long as I sat by it — and half-unconscious as she still was she fell asleep immediately. I stayed watching however more than an hour, and was probably later awake than any other of the Cockers' guests, since when I heard the Admiral and Cecilia come in well after midnight I had still to slip down a back stair, and through a back door, and walk the half-mile home, before going to bed myself.

3

As I'd known she wouldn't, Jessie didn't talk. When Cecilia met me in the High Street next morning —

"Tony never stirred!" triumphed Cecilia. "When I came in at twelve, there she was just as tight asleep as I'd left her!"

I could have said it was at least twelve-thirty, but of course did not. I was only too happy that my ploy had succeeded. (I suppose I was just as fond of success as Cecilia!) And as evidently as she hadn't noticed Antoinette's change of nightdress, no more had she noticed the absence of Antoinette's bedroom slippers — actually still drying out in my kitchen, and which I smuggled back via Jessie next day.

12

So my ploy succeeded; but only partly. Each night (as though she'd learned her lesson), Antoinette slept at Woolmers; but each morning, as soon as she woke, struggled into a smock (often as not back-to-front), and made her uphill way to my garden. —Cecilia took sleeping pills; Antoinette habitually woke before six, and so could evade quite easily. She didn't even need to wait till the hall door was opened. As she'd discovered the exit through my old coal cellar, so she discovered a run-out by way of Woolmers' scullery.

An early riser myself, I was usually at breakfast when she appeared, so we shared it before I, again, took her back, always attempting to reach Woolmers before any guests were about. However the Admiral also got up early, and once or twice we met in the garden. He cocked a weather eye at the pair of us, but without comment. I do not think it was he who mentioned such encounters to Cecilia. I think it was more likely a new arrival, a Miss Ponsonby with a long nose who too enjoyed a stroll before breakfast. "But isn't that child supposed to be *staying* here?" she exclaimed, at our second meeting. I replied, yes. "And does her mother know she's out?" enquired Miss Ponsonby facetiously. The old music-hall gag, as out of place as at the moment her upper dentures, I must say offended me. I feel sure it was she who spoke to Cecilia, probably making some similarly vulgar joke. Cecilia — which I still felt a great point gained — never knew of her daughter's first desperate flight, but she undoubtedly became aware of these early-morning escapades, and as in the matter of the cot took her own measures. As soon as she herself came up each night, she turned the key in the bedroom door. This I learned (via Mrs. Brewer) from Jessie, who complained bitterly of having to knock and knock before she could get in with the early morning tea. Sometimes she heard the child, she said, just the other side of the door — but Antoinette had never learned to turn a key, also I think it possible that Cecilia took it out.

I still saw Antoinette every day, however, for though Cecilia I have no doubt fully intended to be a wonderful mother, she had no idea how much time it took. In New York there had been first Bridget, then Miss Swanson, in attendance; now Cecilia had sole charge. Well, it was what she'd wanted; but not, I think, full-time. What was she to do with the child, for instance while sitting to Paul Amory? What Cecilia in fact did was to deposit her in my garden . . .

Another circumstance Cecilia hadn't allowed for was Antoinette's unsuitability to the whole milieu. Very few children are by nature what one might call hotel-children — that is, quiet at table, polite to strangers, creditable to parents by being seen but not heard (unless directly questioned), and avoiding undue intimacy with lift-boys. With such happily rare sophisticates Antoinette had absolutely nothing in common. Her very silence, undiversified by childish prattle, must have appeared less a quality than a lack; Miss Ponsonby for one, I understand (or to be frank, heard via Jessie), openly suspected the child of being dumb absolutely — which in a sense she was, but Cecilia couldn't have been pleased to hear it said. I felt thoroughly sympathetic to Cecilia in her snubbing of Miss Ponsonby — actually to the extent of asking to move tables to avoid the clack of the Ponsonby dentures. (An undeserved irritation indeed, when one recalls how Major Cochran, under Cecilia's influence, went all the way to Ipswich!) Of course it was Miss Ponsonby who was moved, and she soon moved on altogether, but Cecilia must still have been annoyed; and equally so perhaps by the sympathy of a better-natured fellow guest, who remarked that children of Antoinette's age were very often sullen. (Jessie again, alas; overheard whilst waiting at tea.) Even a merely sullen little daughter did Cecilia no credit; and though she was careful to let everyone know how emotionally deprived the poor infant had been for years and years, there must have been at least embarrassment.

So gradually I had Antoinette with me not only most mornings, but every morning and all morning. It should have been quite like old times; alas, Antoinette was already altered. She had been, in her own way, a remarkably independent child; now, instead of stumping off to squat and brood without a by-your-leave, she waited for . . . permission. Unless I said, "Antoinette, don't you want to go and see the artichokes?" she stayed exactly where Cecilia deposited her — as a rule on the lawn, but sometimes just inside the gate. In the latter event I of course always heard Cecilia's gay signal — "Yoo-hoo, darling! *Nous voila!*" — and fetched Antoinette at least into the garden immediately; but then, as I say, it was only at my direct suggestion that she made off to her usual haunts.

It took me several days to realize that Antoinette also needed permission to come indoors, and more especially to go upstairs. (Then I saw why; no hotel, no guest-house even, encourages residents upstairs before lunch. Their rooms are being done.) Once, at mid-morning, I within and Antoinette in the garden, even under a quite heavy shower she waited for my bidding, before she came in.

"And go wherever you like!" I added — only a couple of weeks before how superfluously!

It is usually when it rains that I sit down at my desk to cast up my accounts and settle my bills, and after such a spell of fine weather as we'd just enjoyed I was more than a little in arrears. I still had an ear alert for Antoinette's footfall overhead, and half expected the heavier sound of the coracle being pushed about; but in a few moments all was silence, and after a few moments more I paused in writing a cheque to the Gas Board and followed up after.

She was standing quite still in the bedroom we had so long shared, staring at her dismantled cot. For it hadn't yet been collected; the Women's Institute was in no hurry, and Kevin, their usual factotum, had apparently other fish to fry. So there it lay, still in its old corner, like a bundle of sticks; and there stood Antoinette, staring at it.

As I came in she turned, and with a sort of politeness, like a guest who fears having seemed overinquisitive, went and looked out of the window. In the embrasure behind my dressing-table was still propped the lid of the big leather trunk on the landing. From being housed there so long it had become like another piece of furniture; I was so used to it, I had forgotten to put it back in its proper place. Antoinette necessarily stood close beside, but neither looked at nor touched it. Perhaps she had done so already?

"Why, there's your boat!" said I. "Don't you want to go for a row in it?"

Permission thus granted, Antoinette immediately began tugging, and I to help her, the leather trunk-lid coracle being heavy enough. But before we got it properly out another gay hail from Cecilia interrupted, as she returned to fetch her daughter back to Woolmers for lunch — if a little late, at least not much later than Paul Amory for the lunch kept hot by Betty.

2

I cannot say it was purely by chance that I witnessed one of these sittings, though chance played a part. —Normally there would have been no need of chance; a mark of all amateur painters is that they do not mind being watched, and Paul Amory rather liked people to stop and talk to him as he filled in the pencil outline of a may tree with pink, or of a chimney-stack with red. (Red was his favourite colour.) But when it came to Cecilia's portrait the change was as great as from water-colour to oils. Paul let it be known all round that he wasn't to be watched, or talked to, or in any way distracted, at work on so important a commission, which as he said might well change his whole life. Thus the garage-studio (everyone liking Paul and wishing him well), was accepted to be out of bounds, and even Betty never intruded.

The chance first operating in my own case was that Bobby Parrish's next bad turn coincided with the birth of Mrs. Brewer's latest grandchild. On however uneasy terms with her daughter-in-law, Mrs. Brewer knew when she was needed, and neighbourliness took second place to family claims. —Also, quite rightly, to those of an employer, and it promoted my always good opinion of her that though she couldn't promise to finish polishing me, she'd certainly stay with Antoinette while I was gone. Why I was to be gone was to deliver a message to Jessie — *"Bobby again, better look in."* When I suggested that Mrs. Brewer might take the message and leave myself at home, her unarguable because inexplicable reply was that she'd sworn her Dad never to cross Woolmers' sill — on the occasion, as I later discovered, of the cook there offering him half-a-crown for a sack of three dozen lettuces. But this, as I say, I learned only later, and at the moment found Mrs. Brewer unreasonable. I delivered the message to Jessie nonetheless, for convenience by the back door; and the back door opens on the old stables, now turned into a set of garages, and one of these now into a studio.

From this point not chance operated, but my own nosiness. Distinguishing, just within the propped-open doors, the silhouette of a wheelchair, I very quietly (to avoid being heard and so causing an interruption) advanced, and through the nearest side window took a look in.

There sat Paul, his easel before him, at his right, on a card table, Betty's marble slab now most professional looking with its squeezes of paint and jar of turps and pot of brushes and bits of rag; and opposite him, on the shallow platform of an old mattress, in a high-backed old chair, sat, in both senses of the word, Cecilia.

I have never forgotten how lovely she looked.

She was wearing the caftan, and drooping over its

lavender folds a long, heavy amber necklace that where it twisted made a depression between her breasts. Her head too drooped a little; as I have said, Cecilia usually carried her head high, erect on her slim throat like a flower on its stem; whether it was she or Paul who imagined this new pose who can say, but undoubtedly it was wonderfully seductive. And undoubtedly she was a wonderful sitter; all the time I watched, she never moved. For some reason I had the impression of a sunbather basking in the sun.

Then through my leper's squint, so to speak, I looked at Paul, who in turn, his brush momentarily suspended, was very naturally looking at Cecilia. —Of course all portrait painters need now and then so to pause, and study, and perhaps probe their subject; but I doubted whether Paul was doing much probing; he was just looking at Cecilia, I thought, as a man looks at a beautiful woman, while under his gaze Cecilia sat a-basking . . .

Neither of them noticed me, even when I made my way out past the open doors — (for my age I flatter myself I have a very light step) — and thus had a chance to glimpse the canvas on Paul's easel as well. Alas, just as all his landscapes were daubs, so all too obviously a daub would be his first attempt at portraiture, and all things considered I felt almost as sorry for him as I had to for Bobby Parrish.

3

Poor Bobby Parrish! Jessie looked in as soon as she could, and was greatly relieved to find he'd come out of his turn quite quickly and was resting on the sofa; but then as soon as his mother turned her back he got up, and slipped out, and loaded his pockets with stones and slid feet-first into a dyke.

It was I as usual when any such disagreeable duty has to be performed who was called upon to break the news to Mrs. Parrish. She took it as badly as possible — that is, made no effort to restrain her natural tears and wailings. (As she slobbered on my shoulder I instinctively felt in my pocket for a paper napkin, but it was so long since Antoinette needed one I had stopped carrying them, and was forced to sacrifice an initialed linen handkerchief instead.) Mrs. Parrish sobbed on my shoulder until the other linen of my blouse clung as damply as voile at an Outdoor Fête, before cheering herself up with the infallible consolation of I-told-you-so.

"Didn't I say time and time again," sniffed Mrs. Parrish, "time and time again didn't I tell 'em, Ipswich was no mortal use? 'Just leave him quiet at home,' said I, 'he's only highly strung.' 'Oh no,' said they, 'into Ipswich for special treatment!' "

"At least he was home all spring," I offered.

"Ah, but he'd still to go back," retorted Mrs. Parrish, "and I saw it weighed on him. I wouldn't say it to anyone but yourself, because you must know it already, but his Uncle Saul was half his life a ticket-of-leave man."

Of course I knew it. There is very little a Vicar's daughter doesn't know of the underground of her father's parish. The implied analogy struck me very much, and as quite possibly a true one: that Bobby had felt himself but on ticket-of-leave from the hospital. I felt extremely sorry for Mrs. Parrish, and gave her what comfort I could by listening to her weep and wail for an hour and twenty minutes before going home and changing to the skin.

No one blamed poor Bobby, however, and the Coroner sensibly stretched a point to call it Accidental Death.

13

June and July are always the country months of sociability. Presently, as a round of cocktail and sherry parties started, and Cecilia enjoyed all the success I'd promised her, Antoinette came to be deposited with me not only in the mornings but between tea and dinner as well — indeed so popular was Cecilia, often after a party was over, instead of returning to Woolmers to eat mince she found herself shanghaied to eat duck at the Crown and Sceptre; so I became licensed to provide Antoinette's supper. In short, after a couple of weeks of being torn between maternal and social duties, and after Antoinette had broken silence to remark "Vermin!" of a chicken casserole, Cecilia generously admitted an error of judgment in taking her daughter to Woolmers at all.

2

"It was just that I so longed to have my babe all to myself!" she told Mrs. Gibson (who told me). "Besides . . ."

The *besides* was that she felt me a bad influence. Why my friend the Vicar's wife repeated this as well was to explain that Cecilia hadn't been actuated by mere possessiveness; but I suppose I must have looked what I felt.

"Not that I agree," added Mrs. Gibson hastily. "Certainly not *bad!* And I'm sure Cecilia didn't mean bad either, in any *bad* sense. It was just that she felt you were spoiling the child, by indulging her too much, and letting her have too much her own way. Do you remember how she never came to Sunday School?"

Vicars' wives have long memories. I thought Mrs. Gibson and Cecilia must have passed, as the French say, some very agreeable moments. I was neither surprised nor annoyed: a friend naturally makes a better subject for dissection than an enemy. My only reason for surprise at these revelations in themselves, rose from the fact that only that morning Cecilia had asked me to take Antoinette back — generously recognizing, as I have said, an error of judgment in not having realized how very bad for a child hotel life was. (Not bad in any *bad* sense, of course; as Cecilia elaborated, just too, too unhomey.)

"Yet she seems prepared to trust me with Antoinette again," I pointed out.

"My dear, where else is the child to go?" asked Mrs. Gibson naïvely. "Until Cecilia takes her back to America, when as she says they'll really be just by themselves together, and Antoinette can have really proper treatment, where else is there for the child to go?"

I replied that I had no idea. —But again I must have looked what I felt, for my friend now hastened to reassure me that everyone in the village knew I'd done quite wonders for the child; only Cecilia hadn't been there to see.

"No," I agreed, thinking of all the paper napkins I'd so recently gathered up. "She wasn't."

"So if she perhaps doesn't seem to realize quite how much gratitude she owes you," persisted Mrs. Gibson — (no one like a Vicar's wife for treading the diplomatic tightrope between a pew-renting parishioner and a potential subscriber to the Church Repairs Fund!) — "mustn't we forgive her?"

"Certainly," I agreed — mentally adding, if it was one's profession to forgive. Husband and wife are one flesh, and the Vicar preached forgiveness every Sunday, but for myself I often doubt whether I am even a Christian, save for the technicality of having been christened. "But all the rest you do agree with," I went on, "the speech-therapy and psychoanalysis and all the rest?"

I was really interested to know. Mrs. Gibson had

brought up a traditionally clergyman-size family with great success, and I was prepared — or hoped I was — to hear her opinion with respect, and even, if it were favourable, to derive some comfort from it. But like all experts, when it came to the point, she hedged.

"My dear, isn't Cecilia the child's *mother?*" said Mrs. Gibson.

From which I derived no comfort at all. But it was a great comfort that from being allowed to spend the best part of each day with me Antoinette came back to spend the nights as well.

3

Fortunately the Women's Institute still hadn't retrieved her cot, so Mrs. Brewer and I between us slotted and screwed it together again, and saw all safe and steady, and brought back the piano-stool extension, and made it up just as it used to be for Antoinette to climb in.

"See, now you're back in your own bed!" I told her.

Antoinette waited. I guessed at once what words more she wanted to hear: they were "For always." But how could I pronounce them so that her ear wouldn't detect a falsity? —When I knew us both essentially but reprieved? So after Antoinette had waited a few moments longer, I began the Lord's Prayer.

At the "Amen" I in turn waited, for Antoinette's responsive "Vermin." She didn't offer it, however, and I thought perhaps she had been scolded after the mis-understanding over the chicken casserole. In any case "vermin" disappeared altogether from Antoinette's vocabulary; having taken five words with her to Woolmers, she came back with four. "Hello! You still have in your rucksack pepper and a tureen?" I took pains to remind her; and punctually "rucksack," and "pepper" and "tureen" repeated Antoinette back to me. Any new vocable seemed quite beyond her; when for "vermin" I attempted to substitute "pretty," for instance, she quite obviously closed her ears.

In a way I was glad: it seemed to demonstrate that even though I hadn't been able to say, "For always," she still felt safe enough to relax from that extreme of docility which had so distressed me.

4

Of course Cecilia fully intended to pop in every day, but at this time we saw less of her. There were her morning sittings to Paul Amory, there were so many parties, and if no official one, usually a little impromptu gathering in the bar of the swimming pool, our American friends and Peter Pennon and the Admiral reciprocally standing rounds. The American swimming pool, thanks to Cecilia, became quite a focus of Anglo-American friendship. —Not that in a sense it hadn't been before; every child in the village, happily splashing each weekend, was fervently pro-American already; but Cecilia somehow polarized it all. On one occasion I was actually drawn there myself, by my new chums the young Pennons, who called me from the garden because they were taking their car and I mustn't let them waste petrol with an empty seat. "Antoinette too," called Janice, "if she'll sit on your lap!" —I must confess I was touched; the back seat already accommodated both elder Cocker children, who were quite large; I felt it must really be from a liking for me that Janice and Peter had stopped and called out; and so I went.

But I did not take Antoinette. As I have said, I had always had a perhaps irrational fear of water for her; in addition the presence of those same young Cockers inhibited. They had seen Antoinette shamed once; I did not wish them to see her shamed afresh because she couldn't swim. But I had also begun to see danger in keeping her too much in my pocket; so as Mrs. Brewer was still about the house, I went.

The children politely squeezed themselves and their towels together to make room for me. They were in bathing clothes already under sweaters and shorts, as indeed were Peter and Janice. I dare say they'd none of them seen a bathing-box in their lives! Myself in my usual tweeds, I explained that I'd joined them just for the ride.

"Don't you ever swim?" asked Janice curiously.

"No," I said. "I can't."

Naturally enough all expressed surprise; but I wasn't going to go into my bronchitis, and left it at that. —Inevitably both young Cockers could do breast-stroke, side-stroke, butterfly-stroke and underwater crawl. They also jumped in, holding their noses, at the deep end. I felt quite thankful to have Peter's backing in forbidding them to scramble over the shingle-ridge into the estuary itself after Cecilia!

For Cecilia was out in the estuary already; and though I reprobated the bad example, couldn't but agree with Sir David as to its being one of the most damn' poetical sights ever seen.

Gracefully, effortlessly as a water lily or mermaid floated Cecilia on the incoming tide. She wore no bathing cap; her beautiful long tawny hair streamed about her like the loveliest seaweed: she looked like a mermaid and the Lorelei and Ophelia as painted by Millais, whilst in her wake and on either side tritons from the U.S. Air Force escorted her back to land . . .

There was quite a competition among them, to help Cecilia towel herself dry before she too shrugged into sweater and slacks in the lee of the American car. —I may say that Peter and Janice and myself and the young Cockers were rather ignored by Cecilia as at best but extras on the scene. However before being driven off she spared us a few gay words, and particularly thanked the Pennons for giving myself such a treat.

"Only where's my darling, my Tony?" she reproached me. "Why didn't you bring Tony too?"

Sensing the ears of the young Cockers alert for my answer —

"She didn't want to come," said I. "She was too busy . . ."

"*Busy?*" repeated Cecilia, with a lift of her lovely eyebrows.

"Dissecting a frog," said I.

So I saved Antoinette's face at least for the moment, at least before her peers. Cecilia laughed — quite well aware, I think, what I was doing, and drew her head back into the car. With her long wet hair toweled in a turban she now looked like Scheherazade. She should have been borne away not in a Cadillac but in a palanquin — or a pumpkin-coach.

14

By July all the catmint I had divided (however untimely), was not only rooted but tentatively in bloom
— not of course with the bushiness of the parent stock,
but exhibiting on each scrawny stem a few identifying
blue-grey specks. (Otherwise I might have forgotten
where I'd set them!) My sweet peas were abundant as
usual, though rather less fragrant, which I attributed to
so long a spell of dry weather; however conscientiously
watered at the roots, only rain, in my opinion, nurtures
the scent of plants; glasshouses banked with carnations,
for instance, smell chiefly of potting-mould. The roots
I kept specially watered were those of my clematis,
Ville de Lyon, late-flowering, but already in plump bud
promising such a claret-coloured tapestry as I only
hoped my tall white daisies might last long enough to
confront; for if there is one moment of all the year in
my garden when I would wish to cry halt, it is when

my tall white daisies outface like Vestal Virgins the purple hordes of Tarquin (or clematis Ville de Lyon). One can see what sort of an education I had had, and I recommend it.

We were happy enough together, Antoinette and I; not so happy as we had once been, but happy enough. She returned to some of her old ways — retreating to brood under the artichokes indeed rather more often, and for longer periods; but on the other hand scarcely ever invited me, by a certain look I knew so well, to help her pull out her coracle. Her affection seemed rather transferred to the trunk itself, the big, quiet, leather-hided animal that lived on the landing; for I often saw her, especially when she thought herself unobserved, standing beside it stroking it.

We were happy enough: what distressed me was that she had stopped making any progress. I have described how she came back from Woolmers a word short, and would learn no other in replacement; now that her riding had been stopped and she no longer saw the Cocker children twice a week, she almost lost "hello" as well; but this was retrieved by Mrs. Brewer and myself saying hello to each other quite continually. "Hello, I'm off now," Mrs. Brewer would address me, or "Hello, I've put the chicken in," and "Hello, see you tomorrow," I would reply, or "Hello, what time was it?" — and gradually Antoinette was saying "hello" again too. But however often we praised a pretty dustpan or a pretty apple, or the pretty Hoover, Antoinette's vocabulary remained at four. —After a little, her fondness for the old trunk gave me a new idea: not with any notion of teaching her to read, but because she always enjoyed the sound of words, I began repeating the names on the labels aloud: Delhi, Simla, Ootacamund.

"Delhi, Simla, Ootacamund," recited I. "Delhi, Simla, Ootacamund . . ."

Indeed it was like a cantrip. I felt sure that if I had discovered the ploy a few months earlier, Antoinette's vocabulary would have stretched to eight. Now it was apparently too late. When by way of demonstration I said "Pepper, Antoinette?" — "Pepper" she obediently echoed at once, and "tureen" to "tureen". . .

"Rucksack?" I led her on.

"Rucksack," echoed Antoinette.

But when I came to "Ootacamund" — not much harder to pronounce, and in itself so fascinating — when I came to "Ootacamund, Antoinette?"

"Hello."

In a moment of disappointment I felt I might as well have been trying to educate the trunk itself. For a moment, indeed, sharing Antoinette's apparent consciousness of it as sentient, I felt the twin brass locks of its eyes regard me ironically. But however disappointed I would not pester the child with repetitious urgings, and so the experiment lapsed, and her vocabulary remained at — four.

I do not often dream, but it must have been in

dreams that for several subsequent nights I heard the words "Ootacamund, Delhi, Simla," then "Delhi, Simla, Ootacamund," pronounced in a deep, leathery voice.

2

Meanwhile Paul Amory continued painting Cecilia's portrait with what I can only describe as might and main; for he often so vigorously scraped out what he'd just put in, the canvas — how I discovered this I will explain later — was quite holed; but he always primed a fresh one on the morrow. He laboured like Penelope at her web; and I for one had as much admiration for him as I had for Betty so near her time there was a bed booked for her in Ipswich Maternity. Though less a friend than Janice Pennon had become, we were always on very pleasant terms, and I thought she took her disappointment over the caftan remarkably well, especially since Cecilia was wearing it to sit in. Betty never said a word but in appreciation of Cecilia's kindness, while as for the Admiral, he thought her too kind by half.

3

We met outside The Chantry — that ever-mysterious, abandoned house halfway up the hill between Woolmers and mine. ("Mine," in East Anglian parlance, designating one's customary habitation. In the unlikely event of Mrs. Brewer's being invited to *mine* by the Queen, she'd have made straight for Buckingham Palace.) Sir David, with little to do in the mornings, wet or fine put himself under orders to patrol as far as the heath and back, and we had naturally met before, but only to exchange greetings and the usual remarks about the weather. Now, however, after agreeing that the summer was wearing on, and that after summer one must expect autumn, he paused, and so of course did I.

"I don't know what your own opinion is," opened Sir David, "but in mine Mrs. Guthrie's simply wastin' her time, sittin' to that poor gallant feller mewed up all morning in a garage instead of takin' proper exercise."

I always felt a subtle distinction between the Admiral's use of "Mrs. Guthrie," instead of "Cecilia," and Paul Amory's. In Sir David it was quite natural.

"She swims a great deal," said I — not quite certain where our conversation tended.

"With half-a-dozen other gallant fellers," said the Admiral. "Of course one can't wonder she's popular, but she's wearin' herself out entertainin' 'em. She shouldn't be allowed to do it, after the punishin' she took in New York. Remember how the first two days after she got here she had to spend practically in bed?"

At least I remembered the note beginning *"Darlings both,"* and Mrs. Brewer saying she'd seen the Admiral about. After so brisk a beginning, even before he definitely had his eye on her (here I refer back to the Cockers' dinner-party), Sir David must have felt himself a bit in the lead, and thus all the more frustrated when instead of tramping the heath Cecilia mewed herself up in a garage.

"Too kind by half!" snapped the Admiral; and strode on uphill.

4

"And the portrait?" I asked Paul about this time. "How is it going?"

"Splendidly!" declared Paul.

I felt however that he lied. In fact I knew he lied. Besides having witnessed the deplorable commencement, I had also observed the Brewer rabbit-hutch newly roofed with canvas perfectly sound except for a few holes scraped as though by a palette-knife. They came from quite a stack, said Jessie, that Mr. Amory threw out. "Threw out, Jessie?" said I. Jessie said well, not exactly so to speak threw out, but he just put them stacked face to wall in the garage going to waste. He wasn't using them. And only two, added Jessie, rather in the tone of Lord Clive surprised, when he considered his opportunities, at his own moderation. Of course she had no right to abstract even two, and even though I always suspected she washed Paul's brushes for him along with the rest of Woolmers' washing-up — how otherwise account for Miss Ponsonby's complaint of hairs, at least not, apparently, human, adhering to the rim of a dinner-plate? Also Jessie and Mrs. Brewer had had sufficient grace to nail their booty back, blank, side up, exposing so to speak neither artist nor sitter, though whether from delicacy or fear of being spotted I wasn't sure.

15

As Sir David and I had agreed, summer was wearing on, and after summer one must expect autumn. Far from attempting to persuade Cecilia not to wear herself out entertaining our gallant Allies at the pool, through August and September I was extremely glad she had the opportunity; for in those months, as all country dwellers know, social effort tends to give place to a general resting-on-oars. With no one's garden looking at its best, naturally no one gives garden-parties; the last Outdoor Fête occurred in August, bringing very welcome rain, but after that in an organized way of festivities there was nothing to look forward to until Christmas. (I do not count Guy Fawkes Night. Though indeed after being so long suspended owing to the blackout, it had become more popular than ever.) So to the period of gaiety that welcomed Cecilia home — and which she herself did so much to promote — succeeded a more typical period of rustic dullness. But at least she had the swimming pool to keep her from being bored, and I fear the Admiral found me a false friend.

However, he was soon able to stop distressing himself over Cecilia's being mewed up in the garage all morning. On September the fourth Peter and Janice Pennon drove Betty to Ipswich Maternity, and on the eleventh brought her back with an eight-pound son.

2

The whole village rejoiced. There had never been a more popular birth, nor a more popular father than Paul Amory. In pagan times, I felt, his wheelchair would have been garlanded with sheaves of wheat, if not drawn by sacrificial rams. Betty took quite second place, but she and Janice, now become her gossip, giggled together apparently unoffended.

All of which meant that for a period of about a week portrait-painting was suspended. Paul didn't go himself to Ipswich, and from the fourth to the eleventh had indeed laboured doggedly on — as he said, to take his mind off Betty. He said it to everyone, including Cecilia. —There is no doubt that Jessie loitered about the garage-studio far too much, and whether to eavesdrop or purloin, the one is as bad as the other; indeed to eavesdrop whilst waiting an opportunity for purloining doubles the offense. But eavesdrop, or overhear, Jessie undoubtedly did, and told Mrs. Brewer, who told me, Mr. Amory told Mrs. Guthrie right out, he was just taking his mind off.

Already an accessory in crime by not having cut Mrs. Brewer short, I enquired how Mrs. Guthrie responded.

"Sweet as honey," reported Mrs. Brewer. "Just like on the movies, Jessie said; rising up from her chair she laid her hand upon his cheek for comfort, and then told how much she'd like to be godmother and called after. Hello," added Mrs. Brewer automatically.

After Betty's return, however, for a week Paul abandoned his artistic career altogether in favour of the joys of fatherhood and, I must say, to look after Betty. (Not that with Janice there all day, and every woman in the village eager to lend a hand, he was much needed, in fact he was mostly in the way, but Betty bloomed like a rose.) So there was a definite break before the sittings were resumed.

Of course Cecilia came to see the baby, bringing hothouse grapes and a toy lamb woolly in cashmere. (I possibly cast a recognizing eye on it; she in parenthesis reminded me that Antoinette had a very pretty little purse, too good to be lost.) For I happened to be at the Amorys' myself, engaged along with Peter and Janice, also present, in the highly important matter of the infant's naming. So nearly born in the Pennon car as he'd been, we all felt Peter appropriate, also such a smooth run up to Amory, Janice already saw PETER AMORY in lights over the West End theatre where he was playing Hamlet.

Or Romeo or Othello or Peter Pan or Charley's Aunt. Or even if the squirming atomy in Betty's lap turned out to be no more than an embryo Prime Minister or Governor of the Bank of England, we all agreed that Peter Amory would fill the bill. —It was a gay, consciously ridiculous discussion — Betty and Janice, as I have said, at this time tending to giggle over anything — until Cecilia's gracious entry made us all behave ourselves. Peter Pennon, flapping like a fish on the floor (originally in imitation of Ophelia), got up; Paul, rehearsing the christening ceremony with a pair of long johns for stole, hastily pulled them off; and Betty and Janice stopped giggling.

"The lamb, the poppet!" cooed Cecilia. "What are you going to call him?"

I awaited Paul's answer with considerable interest. Only he and myself knew of Cecilia's desire expressed whilst laying a hand to his cheek to stand godmother. What made me so certain he hadn't mentioned it to Betty I cannot tell, but I was. However, Paul didn't know that I knew, and so far had a free tongue. So I waited with considerable interest — for here, if he were ever going to, was an obvious opportunity to suggest "Cecil." I fancied I could see the memory, and the notion, pass through his mind — though to be sure he had become a little flushed already, getting rid of the long johns. As I looked at him, so did Cecilia, half-smiling, pleasantly expectant; then he rather loudly replied, "Peter."

"Damn near born in my car," explained Peter Pennon.

"And doesn't it go well with Amory?" said Betty.

"Yes, indeed!" agreed Cecilia — but still with her eyes on the babe's father. "Just Peter, then?"

"Just Peter," said Paul.

I didn't blame him. Quite apart from whether Betty would have welcomed Cecilia as godmother, "Cecil" in this day and age is not only out of fashion but definitely ludicrous . . .

Cecilia didn't stay much longer, but before she left Paul was insistent that the sittings should begin again next day, as so they did, and daily; almost another week elapsed before what was my surprise, walking down from mine to the shops, to see him stationary in his wheelchair outside the Chantry gate. This being set a little way back from the path between bayed brick walls, there was quite a nice little space for him; he had his sketch-book and paint-box out — water-colours, not the new oils — and was painting the vista through the bars. Like all his efforts it was a dreadful daub, but the strong black verticals rather pulled it together, and I had often praised far worse. Only what of Cecilia's portrait?

"That's nice," said I. As I have said, one of the signs of his ineradicable amateurishness was that he never minded people stopping and talking to him.

"Anyway a jolly bit of colour?" suggested Paul.

He always liked using red. But though the roses

were red as — roses, for all Paul's recklessness with crimson lake on paper they appeared no more than purplish. I suspected that he'd put in the bars too soon, probably using straight sepia; the path to the house might have been bordered with heather. However I was able to praise with no more than normal hypocrisy, and Paul looked gratified.

"Actually I've thought," he offered, "if I could get inside, there must be dozens of other angles; *across* the roses to the gate, for instance — so I could still work in the bars."

I felt quite encouraged on his behalf that he at last seemed to recognize his flabby washes in need of scaffolding. —But what about Cecilia's portrait? At just after eleven the sitting should have been in full swing . . .

"You don't know who owns the place?" asked Paul.

"I'm afraid not," said I. "It's been empty ever since I can remember. Someone died, someone whose wife gave musical parties, and now it's just gone to rack and ruin."

"Sounds like something out of Dickens," said Paul.

Obviously he vaguely recalled Satis House and Miss Havisham, though Miss Flyte and the Count of Chancery would have been more apposite. We still had a very pleasant chat about *Great Expectations* before my curiosity got the better of me.

"So Cecilia's portrait is finished?" asked I.

Paul added a curlicue to the top of the grate. (This time burnt umber. It ran at once.)

"Well, I wouldn't say so myself," he told me, "but she's so pleased with it just as it is, she's afraid if I go on I'll spoil it. She's going to have it framed just as it is . . ."

3

I thought Cecilia had handled the situation very well; but with nothing to occupy her mornings she naturally grew bored, and now indeed would have been the Admiral's opportunity to carry her out of the doldrums on the brisk wind of a definite proposal. Whether or not to accept him must at least have given Cecilia something to think about both before lunch and after — for though she obviously wasn't going, in the vulgar phrase, to jump at him, I felt the odds about even. However many strings to her bow Cecilia might have left slack in New York, a bird in the hand is always worth two in a bush, and no far wealthier transatlantic suitor could have made her My Lady . . .

The thought had actually occurred to me before. Neither of the August Fêtes I have referred to was, to my regret, actually opened by Cecilia; our M.P.'s wife, and a local Mayoress, naturally took priority, whereas as Lady Thorpe Cecilia might well have trumped either. She was still by far the most striking feature of the scene, and the most photographed, smiling above the sheaf of gladioli that had been her first purchase. —Sir David at her heels gallantly offered to carry them for her, but not for worlds would Cecilia risk offending the least of market-gardeners. Badged with gladioli as once with carnations, Cecilia swanned between the dripping stalls far more observed and admired than at the first Fête the M.P.'s wife or at the second the Mayoress; but her pictures were printed only on the back page of the East Anglian *Courant,* not alongside the other two ladies' on the front. That any leader of New York society should even notice such relegation in a provincial newspaper quite surprised me, until I remembered how Cecilia with her carnations once hadn't been photographed at all.

Of course she made a great joke of it. —"My darling, isn't this absolute *fame?"* cried Cecilia, descending on us a day or two later. "I must order half-a-dozen copies to send back home!" — though whether or not she did so I never knew; only it was about this time that she began to refer to America as home more and more.

With hindsight I see I might have handled matters more cleverly. The Admiral's courtship was still going strong. He was always at Cecilia's heels, always available to post her letters for her, run errands for her, escort her to the swimming pool; but still hung back from any open declaration of intent. I should have liked to think he was too downy an old bird to be easily caught, but was regretfully forced to put it down to an innocent modesty. Looking on myself — the innocent! — as Cecilia's particular friend, he took any opportunity to talk to me about her; it was like hearing a boy talk about some unattainable star of the early cinema. Cecilia's beauty, which was undeniable, made him feel so humble, that he could offer the title of My Lady as a quid pro quo never seemed to occur to him. He was a delightful old bird, but not downy. —Perhaps if I'd encouraged him to go in and win, perhaps Cecilia might have accepted him and Antoinette found a kind stepfather, and home, in East Anglia; but I had grown too fond of him; and so unluckily Sir David was still beating about — no extra wind in his sails from any encouragement of mine — when his daughter-in-law reappeared to take him back to Richmond.

He went I think not unwillingly. As I have said, he was a simple soul, and like all simple souls, and most Navy types, felt happier under firm command. The daughter-in-law was extremely nice to Cecilia, and after a last (shared) dinner at Woolmers, in a tactful aside over coffee thanked her particularly for all her kindness to the old pet — thus defusing, so to speak, any amorous relationship. (For once I was dining there myself, and from table to table in the lounge one cannot help overhearing.) Cecilia returned politeness with politeness, declaring what a delightful companion he'd been — yet with a suppressed yawn in her voice that declared him also an uncommon old bore. I for my part had the impression that both young women understood each other very well.

The Admiral thus (not unwillingly) shanghaied, and Paul Amory out of court, naturally the whole scene began — how else can I put it? — a little to dwindle to Cecilia. Not only had she become used to us, we were becoming used to Cecilia. Even at Woolmers they became so used to her, she was once asked to shift tables so that her own might be incorporated into a gala spread for the British Legion Old Comrades Association. —Again, Cecilia made a great joke of it, she said afterwards that she'd never seen anything funnier than King and Country, and Our Gallant Allies, being solemnly toasted in Algerian plonk; but the jest, when it got about, was rather unappreciated, especially by the American Colonel (guest of honour), who with his usual delicacy had refrained from supplying bourbon. In any case, Americans treat such occasions with great respect, as Cecilia must have known. I do not suppose she ever expected her flippancy to reach the Colonel's ears, but of course it did, and whether for this reason or another his attendance on her at the swimming pool rather dropped off, so that — to look ahead — the last time Cecilia swam there was in company with only the young Pennons and myself.

So naturally Cecilia grew bored with us, and suddenly impatient to return to New York; and was so clever, and had so many connections, achieved the practically impossible in securing places for herself and Antoinette on a westbound transatlantic flight scheduled for no more than five days later.

16

She came in to tell us quite radiant. Antoinette and I were in the sitting-room — I at my desk, Antoinette squatting in the middle of the floor, her nearest cover, so to speak, the settee. It was quite easy for Cecilia in almost the same movement of swift entry to scoop her up into a close, delighted embrace.

"Word from the airline at last!" cried Cecilia, over Antoinette's stiff neck. "Only five days more and we'll be off!"

By her tone she might have been bringing the good news from Ghent to Aix. (Another poem I had been brought up on: *"I sprang to the stirrup and Joris and he;/ We galloped, Dirck galloped, we galloped all three."*) Only I felt no more apt for the part of Joris than did Antoinette, all too obviously, for that of Dirck. She was such a dead weight in Cecilia's arms, the latter had to drop her almost at once, but still without loss of impetus.

"At *last*," went on Cecilia enthusiastically, "at last, after waiting and waiting, at last I'll have my baby back with me, just the two of us by ourselves! You mustn't ever think I don't appreciate all you've done for her — but just wait till I get her quite to myself and she'll be a different child!"

For the matter of that Antoinette was a different child already. She looked a hopeless sort of child, dropped back onto the carpet at Cecilia's feet and now huddling like a young rabbit bereft of its burrow. It astonished me that Cecilia couldn't see what she was doing — Antoinette before our eyes retreating back into being a little animal. But of course this was the very thing Cecilia intended to prevent with psychiatry and speech-therapy, once she had Antoinette back with her, just the two of them together, in New York.

—"Remember New York, honey? —Well, I guess not," cried Cecilia, "but you're going to just love it!"

She talked happily on. She had the knack, I have described it, of presenting a monologue as a conversation — providing her own responses, covering any silence with fresh chatter, racing on to ever fresh topics before a last fell flat. Anyone simply overhearing (as once Mrs. Gibson across a hedge), might well have been excused for believing it Antoinette or myself who responded, even if by no more than brief interjections of pleasure and gratitude. Of course Cecilia was by now accustomed to Antoinette's muteness, so it could not disappoint her, especially as there could be no doubt that the child took in every word. —"Look at her great big eyes!" cried Cecilia. "Is it like a dream coming true, baby? But it isn't a dream, and it's going to come true!"

All this while, since she'd been dropped and returned to her squatting position, Antoinette hadn't moved, only listened, and as I believed — I no less than Cecilia seeing her eyes widen — understood. Now she rather clumsily scrambled to her feet and took a tentative step towards the french window, then halted and considered the door to the hall, as though casting about for a way of escape. But what I told Cecilia was that it was time for her nap, which explanation Cecilia readily accepted; she was bound for an auction, a proper auction in the Estate Agent's rooms, where she had heard there was some quite good silver going.

I did not want her to leave. I had failed in my duty to Antoinette once before, in the bedroom at Wool-mers, through sinful pride; had in a way failed her again, during the last half-hour, by an implicit, tacit falling-in with all Cecilia's plans. But how could I have reasoned or pled in the child's presence? When any sort of argument or high words so distressed her? I was afraid lest even from her cot (should I be drawn on to speak my mind to Cecilia), she might overhear and be frightened. So before tucking her up I told Cecilia to wait for me; I was going to the auction too.

"Then mind you don't bid against me!" said Cecilia gaily. "You mustn't run me up like bad Paul for my caftan!"

2

It wasn't silver I hoped to bid against Cecilia for. She could have taken back all the Georgian forks in England, so long as she didn't take back a child; for as we walked down the hill together I suddenly discovered this to be the real crux of the matter. No power on earth could make Cecilia loose hold on her daughter; she had too many plans for Antoinette, a whole future had been built up in Cecilia's imagination that centered on the child. (Antoinette so to speak taking the place of Bundles for Britain. As this thought occurred I did not even hope I was doing Cecilia an injustice.) But if Cecilia could be induced to remain in England, especially in East Anglia — especially, I admitted it, near myself — surely the worst of the disaster might be prevented? And it was just as this thought crossed my mind that Cecilia herself spontaneously paused, halfway down the hill, at the rusted-together gates of The Chantry.

Beyond them, the unpruned roses riotously enfiladed a shaggy lawn, beyond which, behind the balustrade of a crumbling terrace, the arches of three tall windows still displayed a cool Georgian assurance . . .

"What a lovely, wasted place! Can't even you, darling, remember when it was lived in?" asked Cecilia.

I told her no, I'd always known it empty: but believed there was a music room.

"The silver won't come up till four; let's get in and see," proposed Cecilia.

With such thoughts in mind as I entertained, I readily agreed. Between gate and post was a sagging gap we could both squeeze through quite easily; though each tall window stood stout to its hinge a lesser entry-door leaned ajar, and within, actually opening off the triple-windowed saloon we found the music room indeed — its frescoes to be sure rather peeling, but still identifiably of harps and violins moulded in what once had been gilt on what had once been white plaster. Under our feet, as we adventured in, what had once been parquet sagged to the point of splintering, and I think we saw a rat, but Cecilia had eyes only for the harps and violins, and as I looked at her upturned face, for once completely unselfconscious, I glimpsed a last chance, suddenly put in my hand by the accident of our trespass.

Cecilia gave me the opening herself.

"But it's perfectly beautiful," she said slowly. She turned and walked to look out through one of the long windows, across the garden. "The whole place could be made perfectly lovely. Why for heaven's sake doesn't someone with money take it and live in it?"

"Why don't you?" I asked. "You've money. Why don't you take it yourself and live in it with Antoinette?"

She had had her back to me. When she turned, her expression was completely changed.

"*Here?*" she said coldly. "*Live* here? Why did I ever marry an old man, except to get away from here? —Not that I wasn't utterly devoted to Rab," she added quickly. "I gave up my whole life to him. But sooner than come back and live here, I'd honestly, darling, rather die."

I believed her; for what she told me was what I'd sometimes suspected. I saw that she wouldn't have married the Admiral even if he'd offered. She had got away once, and now meant to get away again, and no eloquence of mine had any chance of swaying her.

"Of course it's understandable," said I weakly.

"Yes, darling; I thought you'd understand," said Cecilia. "You never got away at all, did you?"

In the event I let Cecilia go on to the Auction by herself. So much scrambling about had tired me; moreover there was nothing, on my part, left to say, as I think Cecilia realized; she helped me back through the hedge with a sort of ironic kindness, and even suggested (my forces so obviously spent), sending Alfred with his taxi to pick me up and take me the quarter of a mile home. This offer I refused; but still, after Cecilia had swung on downhill with her light borzoi-stride, needed to rest more than once on my way home.

I wanted also a little time to consider how I had best, now that her fate seemed finally inescapable, talk to Antoinette. Thinking back, I was happy to remember that never once had I implied any criticism of Cecilia; even such a false phrase as *"Your pretty mummy"* now returned rather comfortingly — for might I not have been oversensitive, imagining that the child too detected its falsity? *"Here's your pretty mummy,"* I repeated to myself. *"Now you're going to stay with your pretty mummy . . ."*

"Now you're going to *live* with your pretty mummy," I heard myself rehearse — as so too did Jessie, on her way to set the Woolmers tea-tables.

"Goodness me, if *you* start talking to yourself we'll soon be for the loony bin the lot of us!" remarked Jessie cheerfully. "Bain't it a shame I can't get to the Sale?"

By the time I reached my gate half-a-dozen such phrases were ready on my tongue: *"Now you're going to live with your pretty mummy who's come all the way from America for you!"* —But what did Antoinette know of America? — *"From all across the sea,"* I substituted, *"just to take you back to live with her, she's so fond of you!"*

I could think of no better way to approach, and handle, and try to alleviate. I even prepared a new version of the Cinderella story, in which the pumpkin turned not into a coach but an aeroplane; and the key-phrase *your pretty mummy* I decided to begin harping on at once, as soon as I got back to Antoinette.

Only I couldn't find her.

3

Her cot was empty. The quilt was still so smooth, just a top corner pushed back, I guessed she must have slipped out and up almost as soon as I'd left her. But where was she?

I searched in all her usual retreats — within doors, under the cot itself, without, under the artichokes; explored the exit from the old coal cellar — no track of Antoinette nor any answer to my call. —I explored the terrace, and every part of the garden, still calling and still without result. Then the second time I went through the house I noticed, as but for my increasing distress I should surely have done sooner, that the trunk on the landing had its coracle-lid on.

Somehow or other Antoinette had managed to climb inside and pull it on after her.

For there she was, curled with her knees against her chin and her hands over her eyes, drawing still a few shallow breaths.

All children like to hide so, Antoinette had often curled up there; but it must have taken much deliberate effort for her to tug up the heavy lid, and maneuver it into place, before she put her hands over her eyes; perhaps as much effort as it took Bobby Parrish to load his pockets with stones before he slid feet-first into a dyke.

She was soon quite recovered, after I lifted her to an open window, and rubbed her hands and blew my own breath into her mouth; and appeared to have no memory of what she had done. However before I went up to London next morning I made sure Mrs. Brewer could spend the whole day in the house, and asked her especially not to leave Antoinette at all alone. Mrs. Brewer didn't ask why.

I made no mention of the incident to Cecilia; but as I say went up to London, to see Mr. Hancock.

17

I had no appointment with him; I simply took the bus
to Ipswich, then a cheap day return, and then a taxi
to Gray's Inn. I was there soon after half-past ten and
(as I wrote on the back of my card) could wait seven
hours. But to my pleased surprise it was only noon
before a clerk showed me in. (The clerk I remember
seemed equally surprised.) On his own ground, behind
his own desk, Mr. Hancock was a good deal more im-
posing than across my tea-table; he stood up, we shook
hands, we sat down, with formal precision. Then he
did something I shall always remember with gratitude.
There was on the desk a little folding leather clock, so
placed — I am not unobservant — that he could keep
an eye on the time without looking at his watch. Now
he leaned forward and shut it.

"I still shan't keep you long," I promised. "I simply
want a legal opinion. Of course on the usual terms."

"Of course," agreed Mr. Hancock.

"You remember Antoinette Guthrie?"

"Certainly," said Mr. Hancock. "How is the bairn?"

"Very well," said I. "That is, physically very well indeed, and mentally out of danger." (I do not know why I used that particular, clinical-sounding term; it just came to my tongue, and indeed, when I considered, precisely described Antoinette's situation; so long as left undisturbed, subject to no mental strain, she was off the danger list.) "She still can't read or write," I added honestly, "but she understands far better, and can ride a pony."

"I should like to see her," said Mr. Hancock.

I refrained from telling him Cecilia had put a stop to it. I equally said nothing of Antoinette's having been left alone at night in a strange place, and her running back through the dark to my doorstep. I had no intention of abusing Mr. Hancock's great kindness in shutting that clock, by embarking on a tale of woe. I said simply that in spite of all these improvements, Antoinette's mother, now that she had returned, still felt that more could be done for the child.

Mr. Hancock considered a moment.

"Without any breach of confidence," he then said, "I think I may mention that Mrs. Guthrie too has paid me a visit."

I was foolishly surprised. What indeed could be more likely, even necessary? And if Cecilia hadn't mentioned it, why should she — thinking it no doubt none of my business?

"Then you know," said I, "she plans to take Antoinette back to New York for special teaching and analysis and speech-therapy?"

"Yes," said Mr. Hancock.

His face, like his voice, was quite expressionless. I put the question I had come to ask.

"Is there any possible, legal way of preventing it?"

"No," said Mr. Hancock.

2

He was still extraordinarily kind to me. He even detailed one of his clerks to give me lunch — at least I somehow found myself, without recollection of any transit, instead of opposite Mr. Hancock across a desk, opposite a very young man across a table with a white cloth. It was proper damask, properly laundered, as were the napkins; evidently we were in some very old-fashioned, very expensive City chop-house. My young cicerone proffered the wine list; but when I asked for milk — shades of my poor father, what an opportunity for *him*, amongst the ports! — settled on his own account for a light ale. However I was glad to see that though my own order, from a menu broad as one of the napkins, was just an omelette, his was for oysters and turbot followed by treacle sponge, all of which he consumed with such dispatch, he easily saw me onto the 2:15 home.

"One of these days you must come and let me give you tea!" said I in farewell.

"I still think you should have a brandy," replied he, rather oddly, "but I've told the guard where you get off . . ."

What he hadn't told me, and what I hadn't immediately noticed, was that the carriage he'd put me into was First Class. Fortunately for my conscience and purse no ticket-collector disturbed what I think must have been a slight nap. —"I don't blame you!" Mrs. Brewer would have said; it being universally acknowledged in the village that a day trip to London is as wearisome to the flesh as exhausting to the spirit.

Antoinette appeared neither glad nor sorry to see me back; certainly perfectly incurious as to where I had been. It was as though she had made a final retreat into passivity. Mrs. Brewer reported her good as gold all day, just curled up on her cot so quiet as a carrot. I had often thought that Mrs. Brewer's similes seemed to spring from quite deep, if unconscious perception. With too much to bear, her last desperate and final escape frustrated, Antoinette was retreating from being a little animal into becoming a vegetable.

3

It struck me forcibly at this juncture how essentially friendless I was. Which may sound absurd: on the face of it I had many, lifelong friends; besides new friends. But my way of life with Antoinette had for the last five years rather cut me off from the old, and my new had their own preoccupations.

The Gibsons were my friends; and had often praised my devotion to Antoinette — so often, indeed, the phrases had become as meaningless (in reverse) as the liturgical recognition of themselves as miserable sinners. Old Mr. Pyke was my friend, and Major Cochran; Cecilia reminded the one of his mother and the other of his first love. There was in fact no one I could look to to take my and Antoinette's part with any staunchness; and it would be no exaggeration to say that scarcely an hour passed without my thinking of Doctor Alice.

It so happened that the day after I saw Mr. Hancock was the day a small memorial tablet to her was unveiled in the south aisle. She had been buried, almost anonymously, somewhere in London; but the whole village agreed (and even backed the opinion by subscriptions of not over five shillings), that she deserved proper commemoration. Even Old Age Pensioners — in fact, all Old Age Pensioners — contributed their mites; and as mites made up the majority of contributions, the result was not a brass but a very nicely lettered piece of slate, recording her many years of service to a grateful community. I was of course invited into a front pew for the dedication, and behind me the aisle was quite packed. The entire Mothers' Union was there, and the Women's Institute, and the Darby and Joan Club, and even the British Legion Old Comrades Association; but not a soul, I am convinced, mourned Doctor Alice as sincerely as I.

"You know what?" remarked Mrs. Brewer, as we

parted in the porch. "You know what I liked about her particularly? She was never one to be bamboozled. Properly sick, she'd get you to hospital in her own car, never mind waiting for the ambulance: but she was never one to be bamboozled by such as that son-in-law of mine faking sheer idleness into arthritis."

I had always known Mrs. Brewer to hold a perhaps unfairly poor opinion of her son-in-law, but in general I agreed; Doctor Alice had never been one to be bamboozled.

As I say, this was on the day after I saw Mr. Hancock; there were only three left, before Cecilia took Antoinette back with her to New York where there'd be just the two of them together.

18

As Cecilia had said nothing to me of her visit to Gray's Inn, no more did I to her of mine. Indeed, I would have preferred to avoid her altogether, though in the circumstances this was manifestly impossible; and was glad, taking tea at the Vicarage that afternoon, not to find her there. It was a small party — the only guests besides myself Honoria Packett and Major Cochran and Mr. Pyke: quite like old times!

We always have very interesting conversations at the Vicarage. On this occasion, I remember, after we had all paid renewed tribute to Doctor Alice, it turned on ends justifying means, such as a crime committed to prevent a worser.

"Such as if I, witnessing a rapist in the act, leaped upon and strangled him," proposed Mr. Gibson.

Times change, and vicars with them. His predecessor would no more have pronounced the word rapist in mixed company than he'd have unbuttoned his fly. But none of us pretended not to hear.

"You'd probably get off," said Major Cochran.

"Don't be obtuse," said the Vicar. (Another change: he was addressing one of his most substantial parishioners.) "We're considering the moral aspect. Would my conscience let me off?"

"Mine would," said Honoria. "Mine would let me off for strangling a man I saw kneeing his horse."

"Then you'd be for it," said Major Cochran. "Not even justifiable homicide."

"Entirely justified!" neighed Honoria.

"What's your own standard," asked Mr. Gibson, "of justifiability?"

"If a chap broke into my house with a shotgun," said the Major readily, "and I chucked him downstairs and he broke his neck."

"Accident," snapped Mr. Gibson. "Not deliberate. Someone justify me a deliberate killing. What about it, Pyke? Think!"

—Again, even if I am repetitious, what a change, to be required to *think,* on any social occasion! But Mr. Pyke, thus adjured, did so. The process always takes him a little time, but he generally arrives at some sensible conclusion, and we waited as patiently as for the local bus.

"Maltreating the helpless," said he at last. "If there's no other way to stop it . . ."

For a moment no one spoke, as I suppose we all at the same instant remembered his father's reputation as a flogger. Then Mrs. Gibson remarked rather incoherently that of course he was quite right, anyone's conscience would be clear, and she only hoped they'd be undiscovered. I always took something home to think about, after tea at the Vicarage!

19

At the beginning of October East Anglia often enjoys its best weather of all: the air, after the equinoctial winds are blown out, peculiarly still, and the sun putting forth its last strength. If there has been no unusual rain the sea is as warm as in August, or even warmer; at Aldeburgh bathing-dresses have been observed hanging out to dry as late as mid-month. So it was now, and there was general pleasure that Cecilia's last days amongst us should be even exceptionally fine, even though it made it from her point of view all the harder to leave. "If that old airline suddenly cancels the flight," Cecilia told Mrs. Gibson (and the Cockers and the Pennons and the Amorys and the butcher and baker) "I honestly don't know whether I'd be glad or sorry!" But Pan-Am remained faithful to its word, and Cecilia was far too conscientious to disarray them by a cancellation of her own.

"Only I've still just got to have a last swim!" declared Cecilia.

Why not? The estuary water was even warmer than the sea; only she should have thought of it sooner, that evening two days before she and Antoinette were due to leave. The sun in early October for all its strength sets very quickly — at six, all still light, at half-past darkness; and it must have been well after five before she suddenly commandeered the Pennons to drive her to the pool and the Pennons (with a spare seat) kindly insisted on stopping for me too. "There's going to be such a sunset!" called Janice as their car halted outside my gate, I in the garden in my gardening boots. "Even if you won't swim, come and see it across the estuary!"

Connoisseur of weather as I am, I always feel a sunset reflects the entire day — redly striated, like a bullock's eye, after a windy buffeting, angelic with small pink cherubs' wings, or, as now, a calm wash of rose misted over with grey. So I was lured. Mrs. Brewer was still in the house, whom I knew wouldn't go, leaving Antoinette alone, till my return. But though the air was so mild, I still scented a nip of autumn, and put on a good thick coat.

The spare seat was next to Janice in the back. Cecilia leaned over from her place beside Peter to say how glad she was I'd come. —"Even though you left Tony behind again!" she chided. With no young Cockers to impress, I merely pointed out that it would soon be dark. "Don't tell me she's still afraid of the dark!"

cried Cecilia. I said no, not if I was with her. "Darling, you've simply cosseted her like an infant!" complained Cecilia. "Just wait till I have her to myself!"

It being under two miles to the estuary, there was scarcely time for more; and once again I admired the speed and ease with which a younger generation takes to water. My three companions were out of their slacks and sweaters, and ready bathing-dressed, within a matter of moments. I was still glad of my coat, however, as I got out of the car to watch not only the swimmers but the sunset.

I had been right to come. Across the estuary, above a band of pearly grey a broader band of pale rose melted upwards into first bluer grey, then into a grey verging on heliotrope, for the sun was already on the point of disappearing below the horizon — in this case (the further side of the estuary being rather well wooded), a dark jagged line as of battlements; which was why there was so much pink left in the sky — the sun not entirely set, only seeming so because the battle-mented fringe of trees masked its subsiding disk . . .

Naturally neither the Pennons nor Cecilia had any use for the pool, but the estuary, though still glowing under a reflection of rose, was evidently colder than it looked. Peter and Janice were out almost as soon as in, and toweling down and dressing again; only Cecilia, doing her butterfly-stroke, receded farther and farther. As the Admiral had said, it was a wonderfully poetical sight, to see her slim arms rise and fall as if swan-plumaged with spray; when she paused to rest and float a moment, the lovely image was of Ophelia. Janice as well as Peter watched enchanted; it was only myself, always more engaged by nature than by any added point of human interest, who perceived the sudden shiver across the estuary's surface that presaged the turn of the tide: where the channel was deepest a few ripples drifted seawards. There was never anything spectacular about the turn of the tide in the estuary; mostly it was a matter of undertow. —*"Tweed said tae Till, whit gars ye rin sae still?" "Though ye rin fast, and I rin slaw,"* says Till, *"for aye mon ye droon, I droon twa!"* My mind is all too well furnished with such scraps of verse, and I could have equally well reminded the young Pennons of Keats' *To Autumn*, season of mists besides of mellow fruitfulness, as suddenly the sun set and night descended and I nearly drowned.

One moment, Peter and Janice told me, they saw me shade my eyes with my hand (as though bedazzled by too long watching of the sunset), the next suddenly totter and take a step backwards into the pool. —It is supposed to be whilst coming up for the third time that the events of a lifetime flash through one's mind: in my own case, it was during that moment as I hid my eyes that my thoughts raced back — and not over a lifetime, just the last five years; I also, simultaneously, recalled the conversation at the Vicarage and looked ahead to what Antoinette's future would be in New York. But my mind remained perfectly clear: and I see it as but a quirk of morality that impelled me to put my own life also at hazard, by stepping back into the pool's not shallower but deeper end, where weighed down as I was to the bottom by my heavy coat and my heavy gardening boots — eyes and throat full of water, bronchitic lungs barely pumping — so hampered and old and strengthless I floundered, I should have drowned indeed had not Peter instantly jumped in and pulled me out. That is, he dragged me to the shallow end, where Janice helped him; I remember coughing up water, and then coughing and coughing again, and shivering uncontrollably, while those two kind young people squeezed my clothes and slapped my hands, and then bundled me into their car because it was no use.

(Fragmentarily, my ears so waterlogged —

"It's no use!" I heard Janice wail.

"Then we've got to get her back, but go on rubbing!" — this was Peter.

"But Cecilia — ?"

"For God's sake, can't she walk?" — this was Peter again.)

For a little way I felt Janice's hands chafing, then nothing more . . .

2

They delivered me, those two kind young people, not at my home but absolutely at the Cottage Hospital, which was probably just as well; I was dried out as thoroughly as a Yarmouth bloater and treated for shock — that is, given a sedative, despite which it seems I continued extremely restless, talking of and wanting Antoinette until the Matron, with admirable disregard for rules, had the child sent for and bundled in a blanket and put into a cot beside my bed; and apparently I said something to her about for always, and then we both slept the clock round.

3

Cecilia's body was washed up next day some three miles down the coast. Lamentably enough, East Anglia is hardened to such tragedies: at the necessary inquest no blame was attached to anyone, least of all to the young Pennons, whose swift action in succouring one of the oldest and most respected members of the community was in fact highly praised: the Coroner only regretted that those un-native to our shores took no more heed of the tide tables on view to all outside any Coast Guard station.

The day of Cecilia's funeral, as I have said, for early October had a curious touch of spring in the air; and now that I think again this cannot have been entirely subconscious on my part, since Mr. Hancock, who most kindly came from London to sit beside me in a front pew, remarked that he scarcely needed an overcoat.

Busy man as he was, he also gave me an hour afterwards — though this I suppose necessarily; for it appeared that Antoinette Guthrie was as kinless as a child could well be, and he himself, in a legal way, more or less in loco parentis.

"Which poses a certain problem," said Mr. Hancock.

I reminded him that Antoinette had always been a problem.

"Which you yourself, if I may say so, have handled with extraordinary understanding," said Mr. Hancock.

I thanked him.

"And success," added Mr. Hancock. "In fact, the best thing I could wish for the bairn is that she might continue in your care. There isn't a great deal of money —"

This was in fact the only thing I had been afraid of, and I told him so.

"No," said Mr. Hancock. "Less than could have been expected. Robert Guthrie indeed earned a great deal, but so did his wife spend a great deal. There is still enough, quite ample, for Antoinette's needs so long as she lives. If you will accept a legal guardianship, she will be very fortunate."

"That's of course," said I.

Mr. Hancock made me a little bow.

"As I say, I can think of no one more suitable."

"Except on the point of age," I observed. "I'm over three score years; another ten and by biblical statistics I'll be a goner already. And though my health is excellent but for an occasional touch of bronchitis, neither of my parents reached eighty; and Antoinette is only nine. Do you know a Guthrie connection, a Thomas Guthrie connection, Janet?"

Mr. Hancock thought a moment.

"There was no Janet in his Will?"

"Which I think a shame," said I. "But he put her through Veterinary College and she came to his funeral, and now she has a practice in Caithness. I admit I've seen her only once since, but it was here, in this house, for several hours, just with myself and Antoinette; and Antoinette took a liking to her."

"And Miss Guthrie took a liking to Antoinette?"

"I've the impression she did," said I. "What is more important, she accepted her. And it's apparently very quiet and peaceful in Caithness."

"You're a remarkably sensible woman," said Mr. Hancock.

I knew I could safely leave it to him to get in touch with Janet, and also felt sure Janet would accept to be my successor; but before I could say so, in stumped Antoinette.

"Hello! In my rucksack I have vermin, pepper and a tureen," remarked she. "Delhi, Simla, Ootacamund?"